Mary Jane Forbes

The Baby Quilt

Todd Book Publications

Books by Mary Jane Forbes

DroneKing Trilogy
A Toy for Christmas
A Ghostly Affair

Bradley Farm Series
Bradley Farm, Sadie, Finn,
Jeli, Marshall, Georgie

The Baker Girl
One Summer, Promises

Twists of Fate Series
The Fisherman, a love story
The Witness, living a lie
Twists of Fate, daring to dream

Murder by Design, Series:
Murder by Design
Labeled in Seattle
Choices, And the Courage to Risk

Elizabeth Stitchway PI
The Mailbox, Black Magic,
The Painter, Twister

House of Beads Mystery Series
Murder in the House of Beads
Intercept, Checkmate, Identity Theft

Standalone
The Baby Quilt
The Message...Call Me!

Short Stories
Once Upon a Christmas Eve, a Romantic Fairy Tale
The Christmas Angel and the Magic Holiday Tree

Visit: www.MaryJaneForbes.com

To

Oscar Arthur Glaeser
my father...

...who worked his way through college
in the coal, gold, and copper mines of Alaska
receiving a B.S. diploma in Mining Engineering, 1923,
University of Washington, Seattle Washington.

I love you, Dad.

Acknowledgements

Thanks to Zoya DeNure and John Schandelmeier for their tips. Their business, Crazy Dog Kennels, provides everything to do with sled dogs: winter tours, boarding, dog sales, Alaskan Store, and the Iditarod. Visit their website (the pictures alone are worth a look):
http://www.dogsleddenali.com/AlaskanAdventures.htm

Roger and Pat Grady continue to dive into the first drafts of my manuscripts mining the pages for grammatical errors and inconsistencies in plot. Once again, their efforts made for a much cleaner book and story.

As ever, thanks to Vera Kuzmyak, Lorna Mae Pruzak, and Adele Fatigate for their initial feedback and catching pesky errors.

Thanks to my daughter, Molly, who somehow squeezes a review of my manuscripts into her very busy life.

Dear reader, as you settle back in your comfortable chair, I hope you'll enjoy meeting new friends and how their lives are impacted by the situations with which they are confronted. Alaska is an amazing state.

The Baby Quilt

Prologue

HE GATHERED the woman in his arms, hugging her tight.

"Are you ready?" he whispered into her golden hair.

"Yes," she replied. Her fingers traced his face—forehead, eyes, cheeks.

"I'll meet you under the south pier … I'll wait for you," he said. He gently kissed her familiar lips. Ardent kisses would have to wait. "Give me ten minutes to draw them away from you, then you make a run for it," he said.

"Yes, ten minutes."

"Helen knows what to do with the baby?" he asked.

"Yes, she knows what to do with Melanie."

Tearing himself away from the woman, the man turned, strode to the back door, out of the house, the door banging shut behind him.

The woman ran to the staircase and on up to the top step. She pulled the air conditioning intake vent away from the wall and then removed the filter. Leaning in, she lifted the lid of a wooden box. A small baby quilt, stitched from various pastels of pink, blue, green and yellow cotton, was folded to cover the bottom of the box on top of which sat a worn suede pouch. She carefully untied the black cord and opened the small bag checking its contents—a gold nugget the size of a large acorn fell into her palm. She ran her finger over the rough surface of the stone and then quickly returned it to the safety of the little bag. Reaching around her neck, she opened the clasp of the chain holding her gold locket and carefully dropped the piece of jewelry into the pouch along with the nugget. Drawing the leather cord tight, she placed the pouch back on the quilt and against a pencil drawing of a landscape on a piece of graph paper. She smiled as she gazed down into the box.

Abruptly she pulled a pair of scissors from her jeans pocket and carefully cut off a lock of her blonde hair securing the golden strands with a snippet of pink ribbon. She carefully laid the lock of hair next to the suede pouch. Pricking her finger in her haste, a drop of blood fell staining a corner of the drawing. Sucking her finger to stem another drop of blood from falling, she quickly closed the lid of the box and shoved the filter and grate back into place. It was now her turn to leave.

She slowly descended the stairs, looking back at the grate with each step. At the bottom of the stairs she turned and ran to the front door, opening it a crack. Peering out, all was quiet and dark except for the katydids strumming their night song.

Taking a deep breath, she opened the door, ran down the path to the driveway, then down the driveway into the street. Suddenly a car careened from around the corner, gaining speed as it approached her. She turned and was at once blinded by an explosion of light. The car bore down on her as she jumped, tires screeching as it swerved.

But it was too late.

Red taillights receded into the night.

Silence returned—the summer night air heavy with the scent of jasmine. The woman lay on the street staring up at the moon with unseeing eyes.

The katydids slowly resumed their song.

Chapter 1

Thirty-eight years later

MELANIE BECKETT, thirty-eight, star real-estate broker according to her boss, was on a mission. The foreclosure market in the Daytona Beach area was booming and she planned to sell more than any other agent. Today she left her professional attire in her closet and dressed for comfort--white capris and a sleeveless navy-blue T-shirt--to canvass the properties on her list. So far her plan was on target—she had checked five of the nine houses and it wasn't even twelve o'clock.

The July heat wave had hit with a vengeance and Melanie cranked up her car's air conditioning before entering the next address into her GPS. A petite, five-foot-four woman, she kept her hair short during the humid summer months, curling forward softly over her ears.

With an eye on the GPS display, she turned right and then right again into the driveway. A low voice informed her that she had arrived at her destination. Opening the car door she slid off the seat planting her jeweled white sandals on the pavement. She reached across to the passenger side, grabbed her tote, and then shut the door. It was only then that she looked up at the house. She took a couple of steps forward, removing her sunglasses for a better look.

Her chest tightened.

She took another step.

It was the house. She was sure of it.

Fumbling with the zippered pocket in her tote, she pulled out a photograph, somewhat frayed and creased with age. She stared at the man and woman in the photo standing in front of the house looking back at her. The man cradled a baby wrapped in a quilt, his other arm circling the woman as she leaned into him, her head lying on his chest as she smiled at the camera.

The chain holding the bank's foreclosure sign creaked as it swayed slightly in the breeze off the Halifax River, but Melanie didn't notice. Hand shaking, heart racing, she slowly lifted her eyes from the photo, squinting into the bright sunshine.

"Oh, my God. It's the house."

She took a step closer.

Overgrown bushes cradled the yellow frame structure. A live oak branched out over the second story, sheltering it from the salty air of the ocean on the other side of the narrow strip of land between the river and the greater body of water beyond.

A smile crept across her face as her steps quickened up the sidewalk leading to the front porch and the door guarded by the lockbox baring access to unwelcome visitors.

Her breath came in short, shallow bursts as she dug into her tote for the keycard the bank had given her allowing her to inspect and show the property to potential buyers. Inserting the card, the lockbox immediately gave way. Melanie quickly removed the device, stuffing it into her pants pocket. She gripped the doorknob, hesitated a moment, then turned the knob and pushed the door open.

Inside the light was dim behind the drawn curtains. The air musty. Only a few pieces of furniture covered with sheets remained—left in place by the previous owner, as if they had gone on vacation, or were snowbirds who had flown to the north's cooler temperatures, waiting for the end of summer before returning to enjoy Florida's fall and winter months.

Melanie walked quickly through the house her right hand caressing the walls as she moved from room to room—a bedroom and small bath, living room, large kitchen, dining room. First floor complete, she ran up the stairs. There were three doors off the landing—two bedrooms separated by a large bathroom. One bedroom was furnished and looked out over the expanse of lawn to the river. The other was empty. In the bathroom, a bar of yellow soap lay in the depression on the side of the sink. A yellow washcloth and hand towel hung beside the medicine cabinet waiting for the owner to return at any moment.

Melanie retraced her steps—down the staircase, out the front door, and on to the sidewalk. The picture still gripped in her hand, she checked again to be sure they matched—the picture of the house and the house that stood before her.

Digging again in her tote, she grasped her cell phone and punched a number. Waiting, she raised her free hand to her face when a whiff of air caressed her cheek.

The ringing of the phone on the other end stopped. Melanie whispered, a tear rolling down her face, "Aunt Helen, I found the house, the house in the picture … my parent's house."

Chapter 2

AUNT HELEN, a woman who obviously enjoyed her own cooking, was waiting at the door. Melanie ran up the steps to the only house she had called home for the first twenty-five years of her life. After a brief hug the woman of seventy-four years hustled Melanie into the kitchen filled with the familiar aroma of her childhood—fresh-baked apple crisp. The furnishings in the modest house, built in the early forties, remained just as Melanie remembered them—stuck in the past.

"I brewed a fresh pot of tea, dear. Now sit and tell me about this house," Helen said shaking her head. "It can't be the one you think it is." Helen wiped her hands on her white apron bordered with pink rickrack. Picking up the teapot, snuggly wrapped in its cotton cozy of red roses, she slowly poured the hot tea into two china cups. The cups and saucers were carefully placed on the green-enamel kitchen table, along with the sugar bowl in the center. A teaspoon next to a white linen napkin in front of each chair completed the setting for her impromptu tea party.

Melanie didn't sit. She paced over the black and white linoleum squares—sink, to back door, to table, to back door.

"It *is* the house, the one in the picture. Look, look, at this." Melanie pulled up the snapshot on her cell phone. "Now you tell me that that isn't the house in this picture," she said, retrieving the photo from her pocket. She laid the photograph beside her cell phone on the table and resumed her trek around the kitchen.

"For heaven's sake, Melanie, sit down. Sit, sit. You're giving me a headache." Helen drew the cell phone and the photo in front of her to get a better look. The photograph worn around the edges from the hundreds of times Melanie had pulled it from her pocket or purse over the years.

Melanie immediately sat down at the table and patted Helen's hand. "I'm sorry. But don't you agree with me?"

"Well, yes, it does appear to be the same place. Of course, it's hard to tell the way the bushes have grown, and I don't remember that tree at all."

Leaning forward, Melanie looked straight into the older woman's eyes. The only sound came from a small oscillating fan on the kitchen counter.

"Aunt Helen, I beg you to tell me about my mom and dad. You've always refused to talk about them, or you found some excuse for not answering my questions. You said you were my mother's best friend. And, my dad—"

"Your father was a bad man," Helen said in a gruff voice. "Came swooping down and turned your mother's head. She was so young … he, so much older … took advantage. That's what he did, took advantage. Good riddance when he ran off after she died. That's what I say. Good riddance."

"You've told me that much before."

"He's dead too." Helen pulled her hand from Melanie, bent her head down and began twisting the embroidered napkin between her fingers.

Melanie stood, walked to the kitchen window, then whirled around, hands on her hips. "Aunt Helen, you must know more. For God's sake, tell me. What makes you think my father's dead?"

"Really, Melanie, this isn't like you. I've told you everything." Helen's face hardened, her words penetrating through clenched teeth. "Leave the dead to rest in peace."

Melanie's shoulders sagged as she slumped into the chair facing her aunt. She knew this woman wasn't really her aunt but somehow Helen had ended up with the two-month-old baby. Why, and whether money had exchanged hands to raise the baby girl was unknown to her.

Melanie had questioned Helen so many times. Why was she entrusted with the care of the baby? Was the arrangement supposed to be for a short period of time? But then Helen had married and she and her husband had accepted Melanie as their only child. When she was widowed, she withdrew from everyone except Melanie.

Looking into her aunt's tortured eyes, Melanie realized yet again that she was never going to learn anything about her past from this woman. She picked up the teaspoon beside her napkin … dipped it into the rose-flowered sugar bowl and added the sweetness to her tea. Melanie stared down at the tepid liquid. She had always obeyed her aunt—a good girl growing up, doing what was expected of her, fearing that this one person, the only person with a link to her life, might vanish. After all, life was not predictable—her mother being struck down by a car when she was two-months-old, her father disappearing at the same time, and now Helen saying he was dead.

Still looking down into her teacup, Melanie slowly began to stir—blending the sugar and the tea with the spoon.

"I'm going to buy that house," Melanie whispered.

Helen's head snapped up in alarm, fear hidden by a veil of secrecy creeping across her face.

Chapter 3

IT TOOK Melanie a month to close on the house, but moving day had finally arrived. She stood surveying the living room. Not happy with the placement of the overstuffed chair, she wrestled it to the other side of the couch.

"I can't believe you bought this place," Alan said. "Where do you want me to put this lamp?"

Melanie wiped the sweat from her forehead with the hand towel stuck into the waistband of her red shorts trying not to snap off a response.

"Alan, I love this little house—my parents lived here. I hoped you'd understand."

"What I know is you didn't tell me you were going to do this. I have plans for us."

"Here, help me move the couch a skosh to the left. I told you why. For the first time I feel a connection to my mom and dad."

Alan, a trim five-foot-ten, lifted his end of couch careful not to set it down on the toe of his bare foot.

"Mel, walls don't talk. Floors are floors leading from one room to another not one person to another. I just don't get it. Until this house thing came along, you were—"

"What? Predictable? If you don't like it, maybe you should leave," she said, pushing her side of the couch an inch closer to the wall.

"Hey, don't get all prickly. I'm sure I'll love it … once you settle in. You're tired. All the stuff from your apartment is here. Let's take a break. We can pick up some Chinese and go back to my place … open a bottle of wine—"

"Alan, I'm not going back to your apartment today. You go on your way and let me putter around. I'd rather be alone. Tomorrow you can come over for an early dinner."

"You want to be alone?" Alan shrugged, planting his hands on his hips. "Great. Be alone. I certainly wouldn't want to intrude." He slipped into his sneakers and walked away.

Melanie followed him out the front door, but the man she had been dating for four years never turned back to look at her. Didn't wave goodbye, wish her luck, or offer any sign of understanding her feelings and why she bought this house. Sighing, her body drooped as she watched him pull out of the driveway, disappearing down the road.

She turned her back to the street, looked down, moving the toe of her sneaker in a tuft of grass. With a deep breath, she lifted her head, and shielding her eyes from the glare of the August sun, she began to scrutinize the two-story yellow building. The corners of her lips turned up and she found herself striding around the outside of the house for the first time.

The structure was a bit of colonial mixed with Florida charm. A glassed-in room, natives referred to as a lanai or Florida room, faced out over a stretch of grass, a narrow road and then the sparkling Halifax River. An enormous live oak, adorned with Spanish moss, stood as a sentry to one side, its large limbs providing needed shade from the summer sun.

Continuing to circle the house, she became aware of the previous owner's neglect. The bushes were vastly overgrown blocking some of the windows on the first floor and even the kitchen window was covered. The yellow paint had faded and a hint of mold could be seen in places, but the white shutters on the second-floor bedroom's double window were in good shape. Turning around, Melanie faced the river. *How lovely to wake up to the sunrise,* she thought. *This has to be my bedroom.*

Her thoughts were interrupted with the sound of a van pulling into the driveway. Thankfully the air conditioning repairman had arrived. With the temperature topping ninety-four degrees, the inside of the house was sweltering and made worse by the dripping humidity.

"Hi. Are you Melanie Beckett? My name's Bob," the man said, grinning as he pointed to his name embroidered in black on the pocket of his white golf shirt.

"Yes, and am I glad to see you," she said with a smile. "The main unit is out back and the blower, or whatever you call it, is in the attic."

"Okay, first show me where the thermostat is and I'll take it from there." He pulled a handkerchief from the pocket of his long navy-blue pants and mopped his forehead. "Someday maybe the boss will let me wear shorts when it's this hot," he grumbled. "Did the unit just go out on you?"

"It never came on … I only moved in today. It was a foreclosure. It's probably been a year or a little longer since the system's been looked at."

~ ~ ~

THE REPAIRMAN made several trips to his van, several trips up and down the stairs to the attic, and a few unsuccessful attempts before the motor turned over. He found the cause of some initial banging, metal on metal, in the compressor outside. Melanie put out a pitcher of ice water on the kitchen counter which they both managed to empty twice.

"Miss Beckett, do you have any filters? The two air intakes are so clogged the air handler won't work right."

"Hang on. I think I saw at least one."

Melanie hustled down the hallway to the attached garage. Sure enough, the front of her gray Ford Edge was pointing at the wood shelving and the filters, among other things. *A lot of work ahead of you, girl,* she thought. Picking up two of the tightly wrapped filters, she hurried back to the repairman.

"Here, do you think the size is right? I want to see where you put them so I can change them, what, every year?"

"Probably more often than that," he said tearing away the plastic wrap. "Let's put this one in the ceiling of the front hallway. My ladder is there, if you'll hand it up to me. There's a latch on either side—I've already removed the old one. It just pops in, snug like."

Melanie watched and held the ladder steady as he climbed down.

"Okay, the other one is at the top of the stairs—easy to reach—no ladder required, you can sit on the step."

"Good. I'll install it while you pack up. I can't thank you enough for coming out so quickly. The house already feels better."

"Sure you don't want me to replace the other filter for you?"

"No, I can do it. How much do I owe you?"

"Give me a second—I'll write it up. You'll have to sign the repair slip and I see you made arrangements to pay with a check."

While Bob went to his truck, Melanie tore the plastic off the remaining filter, climbed the stairs, and sitting on the second from the top step, released the clip holding the grate in place.

"Miss Beckett, if I could get you to sign this I'll be on my way," he called from the bottom of the stairs.

"Yes, of course." Melanie wiped her hands on the towel now hanging out of the back pocket of her shorts, and quickly ran down the steps, her sneakers tapping on the bare boards. Taking the paper Bob held out to her, she walked into the kitchen as she read the charges.

"Here's a pen, ma'am."

"Thank you. How's the condition of the unit?" Melanie asked as she signed the repair form and handed it back to him. Taking her checkbook out of her purse on the counter, she paid the bill in full.

"It's not in the greatest shape, sitting idle for so long. Oh, thanks," he said, taking the check. "My guess is you have several months with what I did today. You might luck out and get a year. Main thing is don't wait until a storm hits, then everyone wants service yesterday."

Melanie chuckled. "I understand, and thanks again." She walked with him to the door, waved goodbye, and returned to the kitchen. Now that the house had cooled down, with the help of the oak tree filtering the late afternoon sun, a cup of coffee was in order. She needed a jolt of caffeine in the worst way. A coffee lover, the electric coffee maker made the trip from her apartment on the front seat of her car.

With the cheerful rhythm of the percolating coffee, Melanie rinsed out her mug, added a generous splash of cream, and leaned back against the sink. Gazing around at the once sunny-yellow walls, she could almost visualize her mom and dad sitting at the kitchen table sharing a cup of coffee with her. *Aunt Helen would love these oak cabinets with the little white-porcelain knobs,* she thought. *The linoleum needs to be replaced. This area around the sink is worn through—the red-brick pattern looks like a board.*

A final gurgle signaled the coffee was ready. She reached over, picked up the pot and filled her mug. Stirring it with the cream, she turned to look out the kitchen window. *That bush needs a haircut,* she thought smiling.

Walking out of the kitchen to the front door, she passed the steps leading to the second floor. "Well, my girl, before you do anything else, let's finish installing that filter."

Climbing the stairs, she set her mug on the landing and again sat on the second step down. The grate hung open the way she left it. Melanie pried the filter away and was surprised to see how large the opening was from where the filter clipped to the beginning of the ductwork. Looking closer she could see the plywood was very clean having been protected from the accumulation of dust by the filter. She then noticed a shiny rectangle in the bottom of the opening. Whatever it was—a box of some kind—it was flush to the front but there was at least a half-inch opening around the other three sides. *If I hadn't been looking closely I would have missed it,* she thought.

She tried to get a grip to lift the thing out of the space but there wasn't enough room for her fingers and she couldn't see how deep the hole was. Trotting down to the kitchen she retrieved a flashlight from the basket containing the few tools she had collected while living in her apartment—the obligatory small hammer, Phillips screwdriver and the straight kind.

Back up at the elusive hole, she shined her flashlight down the slit on the left side. There appeared to be a piece of leather. Shining the light around the back and the other side, she could see the leather was a strap attached to the opposite sides of the object. *Could be a handle,* she thought. *Can't get my fingers down there … I'll need a hook.*

Curiosity now peaked, she ran into her bedroom and grabbed a hanger from the closet, throwing a blouse on the bed's mattress along with the other bedding. Bending the two sides of the hanger down, the top formed a hook. She quickly walked back down the hall and resumed her perch on the step. With the flashlight in her left hand, and the makeshift hook in the other, she snared the piece of leather and pulled it up. The leather was indeed a handle spanning from the left to the right side of the object. Setting the hanger down, she pulled up on the leather strap lifting a wooden box out of its confinement.

Melanie set the box on the landing's worn floorboards letting the leather strap fall back. Scooting closer, she sat cross-legged on the floor in front of it. The box was made of cherry wood and polished with oil giving it a rich patina. There was no lock or hasp where a padlock might have been attached.

She ran her fingers over the shiny top and then lifted the lid. Melanie felt a cool breath of air on her neck as she gasped—eyes wide, her heart beating wildly. She ran down the stairs to the kitchen, grabbed her purse, and stumbled back up to the landing. Sitting again on the floor facing the open box, she fumbled for the zippered pocket of her purse and removed the photograph of the man and the woman in front of the house—the man holding a baby wrapped in a quilt.

Not believing her eyes, Melanie picked up the flashlight shining it on the photograph and then down into the box. Folded in the bottom was a quilt. The same quilt. The quilt in the photograph. Setting the picture on her purse, her eyes fastened on what lay on top of the quilt—a lock of light-blonde hair secured with a pink ribbon, a very old suede pouch, and a drawing. Not daring to pick up the hair fearing it might disintegrate, she softly touched the lock.

"Mom?" she whispered, holding her breath.

Her hand, quivering, she gently touched the suede and felt something hard inside. She didn't want to lift the small bag, but, if she was going to see what was inside, she had to.

She gingerly lifted the pouch from its resting place and loosened the leather cord letting the contents slide out onto her palm—a gold chain threaded through the loop on the top of a heart-shaped locket and a rock the size of an acorn with gold specs glistening in the shadows of the stairwell. *Could this be gold,* she wondered. Putting the lump back in the bag, she then focused on the locket still in her hand.

Melanie carefully released the catch, opening the locket to reveal a baby picture—the little face peeking out of a quilt.

"Oh, my God—this must be me."

She looked up, closing her eyes and clutching the little gold locket to her chest, tears escaping from under her eyelids. Not daring to move for fear she was in a dream, she finally opened her eyes and put the gold chain around her neck and fastened it. She raised her hand to feel the heart lying on her skin.

Wiping the tears away with the back of her hand, she reached down in the box and carefully picked up the baby quilt laying it on her lap. She traced the tiny stitches around the patches with her fingers and then lifted the soft fabric to her cheek. Again tears welled up in her eyes as she rocked back and forth holding the quilt to her heart. At last a connection.

She now knew her parents loved her and had left her pieces of themselves so she would find them one day. She also knew this was not an end but a beginning of her discovery of who they were. The beginning of her own story—their blood coursing through her veins. Today she became a different woman than she was yesterday—one with more self confidence and a new spring in her step.

Chapter 4

MELANIE BOUNDED up the front steps, clutching the wooden box in her arms, and burst through the front door.

"Aunt Helen," she called. "Where are you … in the kitchen?" She walked quickly down the hallway following the aroma of a fresh-baked apple pie.

"Yes, I'm in the kitchen—" She stopped mid-sentence as Melanie set the box on the kitchen table.

"Look what I found," Melanie said with a triumphant smile, "And wait 'til you see what's inside. What's the matter?"

Her aunt grasped the edge of the table as if her legs were about to buckle from under her.

"Here, let me help you." Melanie pulled a chair away from the table and guided her aunt onto the seat. Helen's body went limp, her hands covering her face.

Melanie knelt beside the woman and gently pulled her hands away.

"Where did you get that?" Helen asked recoiling at the sight of the chest.

"I found it behind the filter of the vent at the top of the stairs in my house. Look, look," she said, carefully lifting the lid and laying it on the table.

"No, I don't want to look. It's nothing but bad luck." Helen turned away from the table her body shaking.

"You've seen this before, haven't you, Aunt Helen!" Melanie's voice became strident as she grasped the arm of the woman who had raised her. "Haven't you?"

Helen looked down at Melanie. "I'll tell you what I know. That box brought death to your mother," she hissed. "Now take it out of my house and don't bring it here again. Don't ever speak of it again. Now leave, take that … that thing out of here."

Angered and nonplussed by Helen's reaction, Melanie replaced the lid, fumbling as she did so. Picking up the box and holding it tight against her chest, she left the woman—arms wrapped around her body, staring at the kitchen sink.

Melanie stumbled on the scatter rug in the front hallway but quickly regained her balance. She hurried outside letting the screen door slam behind her.

Chapter 5

MELANIE SAT on the edge of her bed taking stock of the room. The walls need a fresh coat of paint, she thought. Something other than white, and the floorboards need sanding or maybe carpeting would better. After making up the bed, she removed the little quilt from the box's protective custody and laid it over the pillow next to hers.

Now close to midnight, she climbed up on the bed, leaned against the headboard, and took a sip of wine hoping it would help her sleep. Gazing down at the quilt next to her, she caressed the fabric, again tracing the stitching with her fingers. Finishing her wine, she scrunched down under the sheet and finally fell asleep—salty air off the ocean from the other side of the river drifted in her window.

Melanie slept fitfully. Moving day had proven to be full of revelations. Her relationship with Alan, once thought to be safe, was shown to be flawed when he didn't understand her buying the house, or was she just showing her independence at long last. The scene with Helen didn't make sense at all. But the most wondrous event was finding the wooden box holding clues to her past.

Clutching her pillow, Melanie blinked several times, her breathing rapid from swirling dreams. She gazed at the lacy curtain she had hastily put up at the window on a spring rod. Her breathing eased as the curtain fluttered slightly in the moonlight. Sighing, she turned over onto her back and stared up at the ceiling. When she signed the final papers for the purchase of the house, the last known owner was listed as Mrs. Alice Peterburse. She had to find her. Maybe she knew something about the box.

Melanie turned on her side and fell into a deep sleep her mind now at ease with the formulation of a plan of action.

~ ~ ~

A LITTLE after six, the sun peeked through the oak tree ushering in a new day. Melanie felt exhausted and exhilarated at the same time. After showering she searched for her clean underwear, which turned up in a large cardboard box next to the wall labeled *Bedroom*. Grabbing a pair of navy capris and a white silk blouse from the closet, as well as a pair of white backless heels, she finished dressing.

Melanie trotted down the stairs to fix a cup of coffee, touching the grate at the top as she passed. With all that happened yesterday, she had forgotten to remove the grounds. Smiling, she remembered it was while enjoying her first cup of coffee that she had found the box—a good omen. With the coffee percolating in the background, she called her office leaving a message for her boss that because of the move she would not be in for a day or two. She left a second message for her assistant that if any of her potential buyers called she could be reached on her cell phone.

The first step in her search for the former owner would be the banker who finalized her mortgage. Maybe he would know something about Mrs. Peterburse.

~ ~ ~

SITTING IN her car waiting for the bank to open, Melanie pulled out the closing documents. Scanning the pages, nothing of interest popped out at her.

She spotted the branch manager unlocking the glass doors and within seconds Melanie was inside rapping on the office doorframe of the man who had conducted the foreclosure sale.

Mr. Claiborne looked up and smiled. "Hello, Miss Beckett. How was your first day as a homeowner?"

"You wouldn't believe me if I told you, but all in all it was a good day." Melanie entered the small office and sat down on the chair facing Mr. Claiborne across his mahogany desk. "I was wondering if you might help me. Do you know anything about Alice Peterburse, the previous owner … where I might find her?"

"Ah, I've known Alice for a long time, not well, you understand, but as a customer of the bank—enough to say hello. Hang on let me get the file on the house."

Mr. Claiborne disappeared out the door, returning a few minutes later with a thick manila folder. "Okay, let's see what we have. First of all," he said, looking up at Melanie over his gold-rimmed glasses, she's quite old. If I'm not mistaken, she has owned the house for over thirty years. Yes, it says here she also bought the property on a foreclosure—the owner before that rented the house out and died shortly after the last tenants left."

Leaning forward, holding Mr. Claiborne's eyes, "Does it list who the tenants were?"

"No, but there is a note here, stapled to the inside of the folder, that Alice Peterburse became ill, beginning Alzheimer's it says here, and was moved to a nursing home. There were no heirs and the property went into foreclosure, which is where you entered the picture."

"Does that note say which nursing home?"

"There's no mention of where, but it gives the date of October 18, of last year. It took the bank the balance of the time to put it into foreclosure. We had to verify that there were no living relatives and that she didn't leave a will stating who might take over the property."

Melanie stood up, draping her bag over her shoulder. "Thank you, Mr. Claiborne. You've given me a place to start."

~ ~ ~

MELANIE STOPPED at a Subway shop and picked up a turkey wrap with cranberry chutney, and a diet coke and drove home. Settling in the kitchen with her lunch, laptop computer, and her cell phone, she began surfing the internet for nursing homes in the greater Daytona Beach area. Taking a bite of her sandwich, and licking some cranberry from her lips, she called the first number on the list with no success. She punched in the number for the fourth nursing home. She received the same response as the first three: "Sorry, we don't have a resident by that name." She tapped in the fifth number.

Pulling another swallow of coke through her straw, she listened to the phone ringing and waited for someone to pick up.

"Pelican Bay Elder Care, how may I help you?"

"Hi, my name is Melanie Beckett, and I'm trying to find an old friend. By any chance do you have an Alice Peterburse at your facility?"

"We don't give out information over the phone about our residents. But if you stop by, we might be able to help you."

"Yes, yes, I can do that. You're on River Drive?"

"That's right."

"I'll be right over. Won't take me more than fifteen minutes."

Chapter 6

MELANIE'S HEELS clicked down the hallway. She wanted to run but held her emotions in check. Her tan-leather shoulder bag swung back and forth in rhythm with her steps. Clutching a glass vase of yellow roses in her hand, she read the numbers beside the doors as she whizzed by. The door to room 29 was open. Alice Peterburse's room. Melanie stepped inside.

"Hello … Alice Peterburse?" she asked softly.

An old woman, wispy gray hair covering most of her scalp, was staring out the window. She gave no sign of hearing Melanie's greeting. Melanie slowly walked to the woman and lightly touched her arm.

The woman's head twisted quickly at the touch. "Stop that," she hissed and returned to her fixation with the window.

Melanie jerked her hand back, took a deep breath, and moved in front of the woman so she could see her face. Melanie had visited with a nurse before coming to Alice's room and was informed that the woman suffered from advanced Alzheimer's disease; however, she was aware from time to time of her past. This was Melanie's first encounter with the ravages of the illness.

Melanie smiled, "I brought you some roses. I hope you like yellow. They look cheerful don't you think?"

The woman did not respond … continuing to stare out the window.

"How about I put some water in this vase and set them on your bedside table."

Alice did not respond.

Melanie went into the small bathroom to fill the vase with water. She put the flowers on the bedside stand, tossed her bag on the end of the bed, and quietly dragged a chair from the other side of the room over to Alice. Sitting in front of the woman, she slowly put her hand on Alice's hand lying in her lap. The woman said nothing, but she didn't pull away either. Gently Melanie caressed the woman's hands then slowly slipped her fingers around Alice's fingers—holding the limp hand as she began talking softly to her.

"I bought your house, Alice. I love it … the view of the river, the lawn leading from the house to the river, and the cozy feeling inside. There are a few pieces of furniture … I imagine they're yours. You must have loved living there?"

The woman gave no indication she understood what Melanie was saying … a blank stare continued to veil her eyes.

"I've been told you were the new owner shortly after my parents died—" Melanie stopped, a catch in her throat. Taking a deep breath she continued. "I moved into your house yesterday and found something—a wooden box. I wonder if you knew it was there. Here, this little quilt was in the box." Melanie walked to the bed, opened her bag and retrieved the baby quilt. Returning to her chair, she sat down and gently laid the quilt over Alice's hands.

At the touch of the soft fabric, the woman looked down then slowly raised her face to Melanie. Her eyes began to focus. Her body relaxed, and gradually a smile crept across her face.

"I've been waiting for you, Melanie."

Melanie gasped. She didn't dare move for fear Alice would retreat. "Did you know my mother?"

"Oh, yes. Lorna Mae and I chatted many times." Alice spoke slowly, but gained strength with each word. "She was very excited about your coming birth as was your father. He was such a nice man, so caring, so kind and loving of your mother. After you arrived, he waited on her hand and foot."

Melanie quickly retrieved her purse, and again sat in front of Alice. Pulling the photograph of her parents holding the baby wrapped in the quilt from the zippered pocket, she placed the picture on top of the quilt. Alice picked up the photo, her eyes twinkling and her lips spreading into a wide grin.

"I took this picture, Melanie. It was a beautiful, sunny, summer day."

Suddenly tears filled Alice's eyes. She looked up at Melanie. "That was only a few days before your mother was killed, on the road … in front of the house. I don't know what was wrong, but long before you were born Lorna Mae confided in me that she was scared something bad was going to happen."

"She never gave you a hint as to why she was scared?" Melanie asked.

"No, but they were both fearful. Your father was from Alaska, you know, a coal miner. They met each other one summer when he came to Florida. It was love at first sight. Lorna Mae didn't want to move to Alaska, so your father, so in love with her, said he would live in Florida. I believe he was twelve or so years older than Lorna Mae. I never saw your father after your mother was killed. I always felt that he returned to Alaska a broken man with a broken heart."

Tears were now streaming down Alice's face. She became more and more distraught. Sobs racking her body. She began to wail throwing the quilt to the floor. The photograph landed under Melanie's chair.

Hearing the commotion, a nurse hurried into the room. Retreated. She quickly returned and gave Alice a shot in the arm. A male orderly hustled in and helped the nurse return the woman to her bed. Alice began to relax and the wailing stopped, but tears continued to stream from her eyes. The veil slowly descended over her face. She turned her head to the side and stared at the roses by her bed. The nurse stayed at the bedside taking her pulse as the orderly left the room.

Watching the transformation—Alice returning to the shadowy recesses of her mind—Melanie's racing heartbeat settled to its natural rhythm. She stepped to the other side of the woman's bed. Bending over, Melanie gently moved a strand of wispy hair out of Alice's eye and softly kissed her cheek.

"Thank you, Alice," she whispered. Then standing tall, Melanie retrieved her photo from under the chair, and the little quilt from the floor, returning them to her handbag. Shouldering the bag she quietly walked to the door, turned for one last look at the woman who had just given her a glimpse of her parents. But the best gift of all was telling her where to begin the search for her father.

Chapter 7

MELANIE TOSSED and turned, sleep elusive as she played over and over Alice's words: a miner, broken heart, Alaska. Bolting out of bed, she paced to the window, back to the bed, the door, the window. She began mumbling to herself. "Why not try to find him. Really try. He was never seen around here after the accident. He must have left, just as Alice said. Alaska. Alaska. I have to go to Alaska." She stumbled back into bed, curled up under the sheet, and fell asleep satisfied with her decision—she was going to Alaska to look for her father.

The next morning Melanie dressed quickly in her jeans and yellow T-shirt, and within a few minutes was sitting on her front doorstep sipping coffee as she waited for Alan. She had never felt so energized—so full of plans. She'd wait a couple of months, maybe three, giving her prospective buyers time to finalize their mortgages. Closing the sale of four to five houses would give her the money to fund her mission. Of course, she'd have to ask someone to watch her house. Maybe Alan? No, not Alan, he was going to be upset with her. Then there was informing Aunt Helen of her trip. Oh, that was going to be difficult. She had to keep her focus—within a few months she would be flying to Anchorage.

It was Saturday—the day she and Alan always went to the farmer's market to pick out fresh fruits and veggies for their weekend meals together. The birds had begun their morning chorus, and the squirrels chatted jumping from limb to limb in the big oak tree seeming to enjoy the cool morning breeze off the river.

Alan's car turned into the driveway. Melanie set her coffee cup down on the top step and ambled down to greet him with a smile. He gave her an ardent embrace obviously believing her smile was for him, not knowing about her plans.

Melanie quickly pulled out of his grip a bit flustered. "Let me run get my list ... do you want to take a cup of coffee?"

"Thanks, I would," he said, leaning back against his car.

"I'll be right out—the coffee's brewed." Melanie ran up the front steps, picked up her mug and entered the house.

~ ~ ~

THE FARMER'S market was in full swing bustling with early-morning shoppers, the rows of vegetable stands full of colorful produce. There was an area selling houseplants, and another displaying wood carvings. Dad's carried little kids on their shoulders following along with their wives picking out tomatoes and other produce. Some women pulled small carts to handle their purchases and to ease the trek back to their cars with their numerous bags.

"How does eggplant parmesan sound?" Melanie asked as she examined the vegetable's purple skin for bruises.

"Great. I picked up a couple of steaks yesterday along with a bottle of wine," Alan said giving Melanie a peck on the cheek. They both had relaxed—the tension between them over the last few days easing as they slipped into their Saturday morning ritual at the market. Melanie paid the farmer's wife for two eggplants, and then they moved on to the next stall covered by a large white tent with open sides protecting the produce from the hot sun.

"I had an amazing day yesterday," Melanie said lifting several heads of lettuce to find the right size.

"What happened? Here, these beefsteak tomatoes are beauties."

"I met with the woman who owned my house … she's in a nursing home. She's suffering from an advanced case of Alzheimer's."

"What made you do that," he said taking the bag with salad fixings from the farmer and digging into his jeans for the change.

Melanie turned and looked directly at Alan not able to hold back her news another minute. "Her name is Alice and she knew my mother and father and said they loved each other and that he was a coal miner in Alaska and she thinks he's still alive and I'm going to Alaska to find him." Sucking in a breath of air, she held it waiting for his reaction.

Alan's jaw immediately clenched. His brow furrowed over beady eyes. "Melanie, I can't stop you from following the words of a person who doesn't know what she's saying, but how could you believe her? Did you just walk in and she told you your father was a miner, yet you tell me she has dementia?"

"Alzheimer's. And, no, she didn't start talking right away, but when I showed her the quilt she—"

"The quilt again. Come on let's go. I'm taking you home, your house, and then I'm going home, my house."

Dark circles formed under the armpits of Alan's green T-shirt as they walked back to his car in silence. He put his bags on the back seat as Melanie climbed into the car holding the two eggplants in her lap. They both looked straight ahead as he drove to her house. He pulled into the driveway and parked the car. Sitting for a moment, the tension mounted in the silence. Melanie opened her door and slid out of the car as Alan did the same. He took a couple of steps and then placed his hands on the hood of the car looking across at Melanie facing him holding the eggplants, her macramé bag slung over her shoulder.

Alan continued to stare at her, still leaning on the car, his face set in a deep frown. He was clearly frustrated and angry.

"Melanie, I hope you find what you're looking for but I'm not waiting for you while you go traipsing around the country. Not that you've asked me to wait, but I want no part of this foolish notion that you have in your head of finding your father. He's probably dead. If he wanted to be found, he certainly would have contacted you by now. What's it been thirty-eight years and not a peep?" His words dripped with sarcasm.

Melanie flinched inside. He had just verbalized the question she had lived with all her life—why did her father abandon her. She wanted to believe there was another reason other than he just didn't care about her. From what Alice told her, her mom and dad loved their baby girl.

"I'm sorry you feel that way, Alan, because, in spite of what you say, I'm going to Alaska. And, you know what? I'm going to find him … alive … or dead."

Chapter 8

MELANIE BEGAN organizing her professional and personal life in preparation for her trip. She figured it would take her about three months to pull off what she had to do and the first stop was to meet with her boss, Mr. Gideon, the owner of the real estate agency. She was his top agent so she hoped he would be reasonable with her request for a leave of absence or a sabbatical, whatever he wanted to call it. She had no idea how long she would be gone, but expected it could be anywhere from a week to six or more months.

Melanie prepared a list of her clients, charting where they were in the sale's process. They could potentially net her over $25,000, enough to see her through the days and months ahead.

After she confided in Mr. Gideon as to why she was going to Alaska, he had wished her well, hoping she would find what she was searching for. He told her she would always have a job with his agency and was sorry to lose her even for a short period of time. He also said he would put her commissions on the fast track so she would have the money to fund her adventure—providing her with food in her stomach, and a place to sleep at night.

He also agreed that any clients who had made an offer on a property, but hadn't as yet been accepted by the seller at the time of her departure, she would share the commission fifty-fifty with Cindy Glover, if the sale went through. Cindy had been her friend since the two women started with the agency ten years ago. Any clients who had not found, or settled, on a property would be given to Cindy. In which case, Cindy was to receive the entire commission.

Melanie called Cindy on her cell and invited her over for a glass of wine after work, tweaking her interest by saying she wanted to discuss an offer, an offer she couldn't refuse.

~ ~ ~

CINDY SAT at Melanie's kitchen table waiting for her to pour the wine.

"Come on, Mel, give. What are you up to this time? What is this mysterious offer? Here, give me that lighter. I'll light the candle … just get that cork out. You lured me over with the promise of a drink, so pour." Cindy chuckled while she lit the candle and moved it over to one side of the table.

Smiling, Melanie set a goblet of red wine in front of Cindy and then sat in a chair facing her friend.

"Okay. Here's the scoop. I'm going to Alaska."

"If you're going to ask me to go with you I can't. I—"

"No, no, silly. I told you about the box I found—the quilt, lock of hair—"

"Yes, so?" Cindy took a sip of wine but her eyes never left Melanie's face.

"So, I also told you about my incredible meeting with the woman who owned this house since I was baby and that she thought my father was still alive—in Alaska."

"Okay, so you're going to Alaska. What does that have to do with me?"

Melanie took a sip of wine, her heart leaping around her chest at the thought of even the remotest chance she might find her father. "I talked to Mr. Gideon about all this and then asked for a leave of absence. He was very supportive, and we put together how my clients would be handled … and by which agent. My dear, that would be you."

"Me? But you have clients in different stages of a sale and you know how attached they get to their agents."

"I know," Melanie said, topping off their glasses. "I won't be leaving for two or three months because, frankly, I need the money. Once I leave, you and I split the commissions of any clients who have offers out that result in a sale. On the other hand, you get the rest of my client list—all yours."

"Wow. That's more than fair."

"Now for part two."

"There's a part two?"

Melanie lifted her left eyebrow, cocked her head, and nodded in the affirmative. Holding Cindy in suspense, Melanie took a sip of wine and then set her glass down.

"I know you've been looking for a place to live."

"Yeah, I have to get out of my summer rental. The snowbirds will be returning next month and the rent will more than double."

"Well, you told me what you're paying for rent now. How about, starting next month, you move in with me, rent free until I leave. After that you pay me the same amount in rent as you are paying now. As you're aware, I bought this place on foreclosure at a really good price, so your rent will just about cover my mortgage. What do you say?"

Cindy was speechless. Her jaw dropped, eyes opened wide, as she nodded to Melanie.

"Do I take that as a yes?"

"As you said on the phone, hon. You have an offer I can't refuse," Cindy said picking up the wine bottle and divvying the last few drops between them.

"Then we have a deal?"

"You bet we do, sister." Cindy put out her hand across the kitchen table and the friends sealed the agreement. "What does Alan say about all this?"

"He made it crystal clear that he was through with our relationship and didn't want to see me again."

"How do you feel about that? You two have been seeing each other for years. Although I have to say, I was surprised you never moved in with him."

"Something held me back. But in hindsight I believe I thought of him more as a friend. He was comfortable to be with. But, he certainly didn't rock my boat, if you know what I'm saying. I guess I should be grateful for some of the places he took me."

"You did have some fun times. Which little junket are you thinking about?" Cindy leered as she drew closer hoping to hear some juicy details.

"With all of the stories I'm reading about Alaska, especially the cold weather, the weird changes in night and day, and the snow—lots of snow—"

"Have you ever been in snow?"

"Yes. Anyway, reading about all the white stuff made me think of the Christmas Alan took me to New York. It snowed about four inches the night we arrived. It was beautiful. I loved it."

"That's good, because those four inches will be more like four feet where you're going."

~ ~ ~

THE NEXT three months became a blur of activity. Melanie closed four sales, plus another offer was accepted for a couple who were pre-approved, and two other purchase-and-sale agreements gave her three more commissions. Her plans were taking shape. Piled high on her nightstand were library books about Alaska—the weather, the people, and especially the lives of the coal miners. The baby quilt continued to cover the pillow. Each night, after she turned off the light next to her bed, her hand sought out the fabric as she fell asleep.

Melanie had put off the visit to her aunt. She was apprehensive over how Helen was going to react to her upcoming trip to Alaska, but she couldn't procrastinate any longer. Not daring to call first for fear her aunt might tell her not to come, she picked up the tin of chocolate chip cookies she had baked the night before and set out for her aunt's house.

Somehow she didn't feel welcome after their argument the last time she visited, so she rang the bell instead of walking in and calling to her. Melanie heard footsteps, the lace curtain over the window to the side of the door moved a little, and then Helen opened the door and stared at her through the screen.

"Hi, Aunt Helen, can I come in? I baked you some cookies, your favorite—chocolate chip with a dash of almond flavoring."

"I guess so. Yes, come in. I'll fix some tea," she said after hesitating a moment.

Melanie followed her aunt down the hall to the kitchen. Helen filled the red enamel tea kettle with water and put it on the stove.

"I haven't heard from you since you were here last. It's been quite a while." Helen busied herself setting out the tea service—sugar bowl, napkins, teaspoons.

"Yes, it has. Have you been alright? Anything happening in the neighborhood?"

"I'm okay. Haven't seen many of my neighbors."

The kettle whistled and Helen poured the water into the cups over the teabags. She then set a cup and saucer in front of Melanie and took a seat herself. Melanie had removed the cover from the tin and Helen picked up a cookie.

"Um, nothing like a little almond in the dough," Helen said wiping a few crumbs from her chin with the dainty napkin.

"I came over to tell you about a trip I'm planning."

"A trip?" Helen asked.

"Let me back up. I met Alice Peterburse. She's the woman who bought the house after my parents left."

"I know who she is." Helen's face took on a skeptical look, almost bracing for what Melanie was going to say next. "Your mother and I talked to her a few times before you were born."

"Yes, she's the one," Melanie said. *Maybe this isn't going to be as bad as I thought.* "She's suffering with Alzheimer's but when I put the quilt in her hands she seemed to remember my parents and said how much they loved each other and that Dad was a coal miner from Alaska and is probably still alive and I'm going to Alaska to—"

Melanie saw Helen change from the friendly woman who had made tea to one filled with hostility. Her face turned red, lips forming a thin, tight line."

"Alice lied. In fact, I think your father was behind the wheel of the car that struck your mother down and killed her. He killed her I tell you," she screamed.

"Aunt Helen, that's absurd. They loved each other … I know it. I'll prove it. I'm not going to listen to you. I'm going to Alaska to find him," she yelled back at her aunt. Melanie snatched her purse off the table, turned and ran out of the house to her car, tears streaming down her face at the suggestion her father had killed her mother.

"It's not true. It's not true." Melanie pounded the steering wheel of her car as she sped away from her aunt's house and her aunt, erasing the look of hatred in Helen's eyes.

"I'll prove that they loved each other ... and me."

Chapter 9

Anchorage, Alaska

THE PLANE dipped a wing circling to land at Ted Stevens International Airport in Anchorage. Melanie, a breath away from the glass of her window, strained to look out in all directions. The Anchorage skyline, framed by the plane's window, was a masterpiece. Now dusk, the panes of glass on the skyscraper silhouettes standing at the water's edge were painted with gold, reflecting on the dark blue, inky waters of Cook Inlet. Rising majestically behind the silhouettes were the mountains, the peaks painted with more gold from the setting sun's rays.

Melanie felt the city reaching out to her in a most spectacular welcome. It was love at first sight. The stewardess, reading from a weather bulletin, said that dawn would begin at 7:01 tomorrow with sunrise at 9:31 and set at 5:55 p.m. with the prolonged light of dusk of over an hour.

Melanie quickly turned her watch back four hours to 6:21 p.m. It was proving to be a long day. Flying out of Orlando, she had chased the sun from east to west—traveling over eighteen hours. Deplaning, she was hit with a blast of frigid air. Alaskan's might call eighteen degrees mild for the first of November, but leaving Orlando, where many wore shorts and flip-flops, the cold air was a shock.

Melanie picked up her suitcases and then followed the signs to the car rental counter. Verifying the car had a GPS device, she thanked the agent and picked up the keys along with a detailed street map of Anchorage, and a general map of the surrounding towns. The maps would be added to the other information she had collected over the last three months preparing for her trip. The car-rental lady had said that she might encounter a few snow flurries, but no accumulation was expected and as of now the skies were clear. Over the last week, however, a foot of the white stuff had fallen on the city.

Pulling away from the airport, Melanie was soon on 6th Avenue which became AK-1 heading east out of town to Palmer. Reading the signs, AK-1 was posted as Glenn Highway, speed limit 65 miles-per-hour. The department in charge of shoveling the roads knew their business—the highway was clear and dry with a few snow banks off the shoulders. She had made reservations at the Eagles Nest, a bed and breakfast lodge in Palmer, situated forty-three miles east of Anchorage but a short hop of thirty minutes to her first destination tomorrow—Houston.

Melanie was making good time on the highway—thankfully there wasn't much traffic. Opening her car window a crack, Melanie breathed in the cold, crisp air. Night had fully descended laying a blanket of twinkling stars in the sky. The snow-covered mountains glistened faintly in the moonlight. *God, it's beautiful here,* she thought.

Looking down at the printout in her hand, if the MapQuest directions were accurate, she would be at the lodge in less than an hour. Being a realtor, she had become an expert at finding her destinations, and with a GPS it was a no-brainer. Thinking it would be a good idea to let the innkeeper know she was on her way, Melanie pulled off the road but kept the motor running and the heater turned on high.

She scanned the numbers she had stored when making her trip arrangements—the Department of Interior with information on the coal mines she might visit, and the Eagles Nest. She had picked the lodge because it seemed to be in the center of several mining towns, or at least within a day's trip in any direction. Selecting the number for the lodge, a woman picked up on the first ring.

"Eagles Nest, Cathy Erlick, may I help you?"

"Hi, Cathy. This is Melanie Beckett. Just wanted to let you know my flight was on time and I figure I'm twenty or so minutes away."

"Wonderful, Melanie. We're ready for you. Give a honk when you pull in and Tom will come out to help with your luggage."

Looking out of the corners of her eyes she caught another glimpse of the spectacular mountain range to the north. For a girl who grew up in the rolling hills of Florida, the mountains looked immense as they pierced the moonlit sky. It seemed no time at all when she spotted the first sign for the lodge. She navigated the turn off the highway and was happy to see the Eagle Nest sign ablaze with floodlights pointing the way to the driveway leading up to the lodge.

The Eagles Nest was a large log cabin with several wings extending off of each side. Floodlights in the parking lot bounced off the snow banks—the scene picturesque and inviting. Tom hustled out the front entrance struggling to stick his arms through the sleeves of his parka. He greeted Melanie with a firm handshake and then snatched her bags out of the trunk.

Inside she was greeted with a warm fire in the stone fireplace—the stones rising to the top of the cathedral ceiling, the flames casting a glow over the log walls. Large, red oriental rugs were placed in the center of various seating areas inviting conversation.

The owners of the lodge, Cathy and Tom Erlick, were as warm and thoughtful in person as they had been in taking her reservation. They had been intrigued with her story and told her they would help in any way they could with her search.

While Tom took her bags up to her room, Cathy insisted she have a cup of hot cocoa before turning in. Their other guests had already gone to their rooms for the night. It was ten o'clock. By Florida time Melanie had now been up for over twenty-two hours.

~ ~ ~

MELANIE OPENED her eyes. It was dark gray out so she snuggled back under the covers still feeling a bit groggy. Picking up the clock on the bedside table, she checked the time. It was 8:34

and the scent of bacon and eggs drifted under the door. She closed her eyes again. *Wait a minute,* she thought. *It's morning but the sun isn't up yet.* She jumped out of bed, freshened up, and pulled on her hose, brown slacks, and pulled on a tan sweater over her white turtleneck shirt. Stuffing her feet into her brown pumps, she then stepped to the bathroom vanity. Fluffing up her blonde hair, applying lipstick and a little eyeliner, she took a last appraising look at herself in the bathroom mirror. "Not bad for covering over 4000 miles yesterday," she said to her reflection.

Following the aroma of the coffee service on the small table in the hallway, Melanie poured herself a cup and entered the dining room. The room was cozy with a crackling fire and muted tones of a Vivaldi concerto. A couple was helping themselves to the breakfast buffet and Melanie queued up behind them.

"How long have you two been up? I'm not used to the sun rising so late," Melanie said laughing.

The couple laughed along with her. They took their plates to a long, pine harvest table in front of a wall of windows giving a panoramic view of the mountains. There were a few smaller unoccupied tables against the far wall. Cathy didn't mention last night how many guests were staying at the lodge. Melanie, spotting a newspaper, decided to go to the opposite end of the long table. Taking a sip of coffee, she was beginning to feel better already. She heard a man talking to Cathy in the hallway as he fixed his coffee. He gave a chuckle and then entered the dining room and continued on to the buffet.

Melanie usually didn't stare at a man or anyone for that matter. But this stranger seemed to fill the room with his presence, yet he hadn't said a word other than his brief conversation in the hall with Cathy. He was tall, sandy-red hair, and a physique that yelled five-star physical fitness routine.

He turned from the buffet with his plate of scrambled eggs, wheat toast, and melon wedges in one hand and his coffee in the other. His reaction at the sight of Melanie sitting at the table was to stare back at her. Recovering, he sauntered over and sat opposite her at the table. Setting his plate and coffee down, he leaned across the table offering her his hand.

"My name is Mitch O'Reilly. May I ask your name?"

"Pleased to meet you, Mr. O'Reilly. I'm Melanie Beckett," she said shaking his hand and then leaning back in her chair.

"Miss Melanie Beckett?"

"Yes, Miss."

"I didn't see you last night at dinner. You must have arrived late," Mitch said, taking a sip of coffee.

"It was late. It had been a long day."

"You sound like you're from one of the lower 48."

"Yup, all the way from Orlando to Anchorage. I flew into Anchorage late yesterday and then drove up here to the lodge."

"Orlando? Florida?"

"Florida! I'll tell you, stepping off the plane was quite a shock," she said with a wide smile.

"And now you're here in Palmer, Alaska. There has to be quite a story to bring you so far."

"There is. I'm meeting with someone in Houston at 11:30."

"Well, I'm headed to Houston myself. I have a few appointments there. Tell you what, I'd be glad to drive, drop you off at your appointment, and then how about meeting later for a beer or whatever you'd like to drink. There's a terrific old bar in Houston—"

"That's very nice of you, but I don't want to put you out, and I'm not exactly sure how long my—"

"Put me out? You'll save me from talking to myself. I'm not a very good conversationalist."

"I'd say you're pretty good … at conversation," Melanie said, smiling as a little color rose in her cheeks.

"If you don't mind my asking, who are you meeting in Houston," Mitch said. "There are only a couple thousand people who claim to be residents."

"Mr. Swenson at the Chamber of Commerce."

"So, Gary is the lucky man."

Cathy strolled around the table topping of her guest's coffee cups. "Dr. O'Reilly, would you like a little more coffee?"

"You know I would—always takes two cups before I can really function in the morning," he said, flashing Cathy a friendly smile. He looked back at Melanie who had one eyebrow raised.

"Oops, I guess Cathy blew my cover. Yes, I'm a doctor."

"What field?"

"Respiratory. So getting back to my offer. Can I escort you to Houston? It's only a little over thirty minutes from here. I'll drop you off at the chamber and then we can rendezvous later for a beer in the beer hall. Do you have a cell?"

Melanie nodded, yes, as she took a bite of toast slathered with orange marmalade jam.

"Good. Let's swap numbers. Then if you finish early you can give me a call. My time is very flexible. But if I know Gary, he'll take up most of your afternoon. Oh, there's one more thing, or maybe two."

"And what's that?" Melanie loved every bit of the by-play with Mitch O'Reilly. He was very charming and she was delighted with his offer to drive to Houston.

"Over the beer, you have to tell me why you came all the way from Florida to meet with a chamber guy in Houston, Alaska. And, number two, where did you get that locket? It's very pretty."

Chapter 10

Houston, Alaska

MELANIE WRAPPED a red-plaid scarf around her neck and cinched in the belt of her tan car coat. Picking up her laptop and briefcase, she left her room and went to meet Mitch at the lodge's front entrance. He was waiting for her and guided her to his black SUV.

"Hope you like dogs," he said.

As they approached the car she heard a sad howling sound.

"Love dogs. Why?"

"Hear that … that's Nikita. I put her in the car five minutes ago and she already has separation anxiety. Wait here while I let her out to meet you."

Mitch opened the back of the car and a very exuberant dark-gray and white husky jumped out, dashed around the parking lot twice, then came and sat in front of her master, tongue hanging out, smiling.

"Niki, this is Melanie. Shake hands like a good girl."

Melanie put her briefcase down on the cement and clasped Niki's paw which was fanning the air in front of her. Melanie, leaning over, also received a lick on the cheek. Niki, introduction over, performed another quick lap of the parking lot and then jumped in the back of the car at Mitch's command.

"She's a beauty, and what a bundle of energy," Melanie said, picking up her briefcase and sliding into the car's passenger seat. Mitch tucked in her coat and closed the door.

"That bundle of energy," Mitch replied as he climbed in behind the wheel, "drives me a bit crazy. One of my patients couldn't keep her any longer and begged me to take her. She's a sled dog, that is, she's a sled dog in training. I don't have enough time to exercise her properly or to train her. That's one reason she's riding with us today. There's a guy with a sled team in Houston. He said he'd take her for a couple of weeks, work with her, and see how she does with his team. Find out what position on the team might suit her."

Melanie turned around to get another look at Niki. Mitch had installed a woven leather barrier between the front and back seats so the dog couldn't jump up and join them.

"Her eyes—one brown and one blue?"

"Yeah, it's not unusual—two ice blue, or one of each, half blue and half brown known as parti-eyed, both brown—you name it."

Thirty minutes later Mitch pulled to a stop.

"That's the chamber's building. There's a receptionist just inside the door. Let's make sure we have our correct numbers, he said. Melanie dug inside a pocket of her briefcase and handed Mitch her business card.

"Ah, you're a real-estate agent. Did you come 4000 miles to buy a house?" he asked smiling.

"Not exactly. Thanks for the ride. My meeting shouldn't take more than a couple of hours—how about you?"

"Couple of hours sounds good. I won't call you, unless I think old Gary is making a pest of himself. Let me know when you're finished and I'll pick you up."

Melanie waved goodbye and walked up to the front door of the small, frame building weathered with age.

~ ~ ~

OLD MR. SWENSON, as Mitch put it, was about forty-five, fit, and friendly. They sat across the table from each other, a table that looked like it had seen many battles over the years. The table and six chairs were the only pieces of furniture in the room which needed a coat of paint. They each had a cup of coffee in front of them—Melanie warming her fingers around the mug.

"Mr. Swenson—"

"Oh, please call me Gary."

"Gary. Were you able to find any information on my father?"

"I must say, Melanie ... may I call you Melanie?"

"Of course."

"After you called last month, I did some digging. We have a historical society here. Very dedicated people. We're a small borough—only sixteen miles from Wasilla. Once Sarah Palin burst on the scene, everyone perks up when you mention Wasilla." Gary laughed as he rolled his eyes. "How about another cup of coffee, Melanie?"

"Yes, please. It's nice and hot." Melanie hoped he would get to her request for information soon. Of course, like most leaders of a local chamber, he wanted to sell his town.

Gary stepped out of the room and returned shortly with a fresh carafe of coffee.

"As I was saying, several coal mines were developed in our area around 1917. Houston's coal was used extensively by the U.S. Navy right up through WWII. Mind you, from 1949 to 1952 over 65,000 tons of coal was mined right here."

Gary stopped a moment, took a sip of coffee and then walked to a large, framed map attached to the wall. "Right here," he said tapping a spot on the map. "Our coal." He returned to his chair at the table.

"Then the war ended and they shut the mine down a few years later, around '52."

"That must have been devastating to the town," Melanie said, adding a dash more coffee to both of their cups.

"Yeah, over fifty years ago, but we're coming back—some of the best hunting and fishing happens in these parts. Tourists flock here in the summer."

"Gary, you mentioned on the phone that you'd see if you could find any record of my father, working or living here."

"Melanie, I checked with the historical society and they made some calls to the old timers, because from what you said, your father would be over seventy now—why he'd be in his prime," Gary said with a smile. "Providing, that is, that he didn't have the black lung."

"Black lung is bad."

"Yeah. Miners came down with the disease from breathing in the coal dust. But, anyway, I'm afraid we have no record of an Arthur Beckett."

The receptionist walked into the conference room and handed Mr. Swenson a note. He thanked her and then turned to Melanie.

"It seems Dr. O'Reilly is here to pick you up."

Melanie checked her watch and was surprised that a couple of hours had passed. "Gary, I didn't realize … you've been most generous with your time." She stood, picked up her coat, but Swenson quickly stepped to help her with the garment.

"I wish I could have been more help," he said. "If I come across anything about your father, I'll certainly give you a call. I have a couple of ideas on where else I might look."

"Thank you. Here's my cell number," Melanie said, handing him her business card.

Swenson walked with Melanie into the reception area and, smiling broadly, greeted Mitch with a hearty handshake.

"Nice to see you, Doctor. Miss Beckett and I have had a lovely chat, but sadly I wasn't able to help her."

"I'm sure you tried, Gary." Turning to Melanie, Mitch said, "I hope you don't mind my coming for you. I finished a little early with the patients I had to see."

"No, you didn't interrupt. Gary and I had finished." Turning to Mr. Swenson Melanie extended her hand and thanked him again for his time.

Chapter 11

FLURRIES SWIRLED around the cars in the parking lot. Mitch kept a firm grip on Melanie's elbow so she wouldn't fall where the pavement was beginning to ice up. Safely settling her in the front seat, he hurried around to the other side pulling his parka tight around his neck against the cold wind. Leaving the parking lot, he looked over at Melanie who was grinning at him.

"Gary Swenson was very nice, a real gentleman, just in case you were wondering."

"Never crossed my mind," he said grinning back at her. "However, Gary said he couldn't help you with whatever it was you needed help with, which can only mean you'll be staying in the area a little while longer. These flurries may not amount to much, but you never can tell what Mother Nature has up her parka for us. So, my Florida friend, we are going shopping after which we will get that beer I promised and your story that you promised."

"I don't recall promising you a story."

"Hey, did you or did you not accept the terms of my driving you to Houston?"

"Well, if you put it that way, I guess I did."

A few minutes later, Mitch pulled up in front of an old-fashioned clothing store built of logs. An extension of the roof over the front porch provided cover for a few chairs provided for shoppers to rest when the weather allowed. Here and there spittoons were strategically placed presumably for the old timers while they told their tales of their mine adventures.

An hour later Melanie and Mitch exited, laughing at her makeover—heavy suede boots lined with lamb's wool, and a red, nylon-quilted down parka with fur surrounding her face. Juggling her purchases, including a pair of long johns, they scurried to the car.

"I don't know about you, but I have worked up a terrible thirst. I didn't realize how hard it is to dress a child."

"Excuse me. A child?"

"Yeah. You should have seen your face when you opened the trap door of that pair of underwear," he said, piling the bundles in the back seat as she climbed into the car. Still laughing he jumped into the seat beside her, shut his door, and turned the key in the ignition.

"We have quite a ride before we get to the saloon," he warned her as he made a U-turn. They both laughed as he pulled into a parking place across the street from the clothing store.

The bar was in yet another log building. The walls were lined with pictures of miners, their faces covered with coal dust. Interspersed with the pictures were heads of moose, deer, and caribou. Various species of birds were perched on the wooden beams.

Mitch guided her to a table by the window and helped her remove her parka. A pretty red-haired waitress hustled up to take their order setting two glasses of ice water on the table.

"Dr. O'Reilly, bout time you came in to see me. Brought a pretty lady with you this time, I see."

"Now, now, Millie, don't you go and get all jealous. You know you're the only girl for me."

"Oh, doc, how you go on. I'm just teasing, miss. You're the first lady he's ever brought in here. Now, what can I get you two?"

"Melanie, order what you like—this is a full-service bar," Mitch said in a serious tone.

"You order for me, please ... until I learn the ropes that is," Melanie replied with a twinkle in her eye and a wink at Millie.

"Something to drink?"

"Two Glacier brews, if you please. Want to introduce the lady to a real Anchorage micro-brewed beer."

"And, will you be wanting anything to eat?"

"Depends, my dear, on what the proprietor bagged this morning—deer, I think not, but a grizzly steak could tempt me—not sure about this Florida girl, however."

"Oh, brother, you're fired up today," Millie said looking skyward with a smile as she laid a couple of menus on the table and scampered off to get the beers.

"Now, Miss Beckett, that you are dressed for the beginning of winter, you will soon taste the best beer in Alaska, although there are a couple of rivals. And, it is *your turn* to tell me why you've come all these miles to visit Mr. Gary Swenson."

Melanie pulled an empty chair up between Mitch and her and plopped her large tote down. Opening the bag, she felt around for the zippered pocket and retrieved the picture of her mother and father holding a baby in front of the house she now owned. She related to Mitch the story about her mother being killed in a hit-and-run accident, her father disappearing, and how thirty-eight years later she came across the same house and bought it. She told him that on the day she moved in she found a wooden box in the air conditioning vent. She also filled him in on her Aunt Helen, who had raised her, and how the woman displayed a deep hatred for her father, blaming him for her mother's death.

Millie had placed two glasses and the bottles of beer on the table. Mitch added to her glass from time to time, never asking her if she wanted more fearing he might interrupt the story pouring from her heart. He made a hand-signal to Millie at one point which Millie correctly interpreted as two orders for his usual steak, baked potato with the fixings, and one more beer.

"Then I looked up the woman, Alice Peterburse, who had purchased the house vacated by my parents. Honest to God, Mitch, it was amazing. She has advanced Alzheimer's, and I—" Melanie stopped talking a moment. Digging to the bottom of her bag, she retrieved the little quilt. "Alice all of a sudden came out of her black hole and started to talk. She recognized this quilt, and told me my father loved my mother very much— something that Helen would never agree with—and, that he came from the mines in Alaska, swept my mother off her feet, and … and … that's all I know … and here I am." A tear slid down her cheek as she finished her story.

Mitch picked up his napkin and gently blotted the runaway tear. Giving Melanie time to compose herself, he fixed his potato and hers, each time questioning with a nod and raised brows if she wanted the pat of butter, the scoop of sour cream and bacon bits. She nodded, yes, to each of his questions and finally let out a sigh.

"I'm okay now. Thank you."

"The locket you're wearing—looks the same as the one in the picture."

"It is the same. It was in the pouch with the rock," Melanie replied.

"How did you happen to pick Houston as a starting point?"

"I contacted the Department of the Interior in Juneau. I could be wrong, but I figure my father would be around seventy-five now, and Alice said he was a miner, so, maybe he worked in the mines fifty or so years ago. The department gave me a list of potential mining towns. Houston was on the list and closest to the Anchorage Airport. Don't ask me why I flew into Anchorage instead of Juneau. I can't tell you why. I'm probably on a fool's mission—so much time has lapsed …" another tear escaped her eye. This time she wiped it away with the back of her hand.

"I'm sorry. I usually keep my emotions in check. I'm probably just tired from the trip yesterday … and then you … well you've been so kind. It's been a wonderful day, really," she said bathing him in a warm smile and swiping another tear away. She took a sip of beer, closed her eyes, willing herself to get a grip. She opened her eyes feeling his stare—his face displayed concern, but also warmth toward a new friend in need of someone to believe in her. He leaned across the chair between them which held her bag, and kissed her gently on the cheek.

"I'll help you find your father, Melanie." His voice was husky. He turned away from her and looked out the window, lifting his water glass to his lips as he did so.

What just happened, she wondered.

Turning back, he looked into her eyes and saw surprise.

To break the tension, Melanie attacked her steak. Mitch laughed as he took a forkful of buttered potato.

"What's that other piece of paper you had folded around the picture of your house?"

"Oh, let me get it out—it was also in the box I found. She wiped a spot on the table with her napkin to be sure it was clean and then laid the pen and ink drawing down smoothing out the creases. "I presume either my mom or my dad drew it, but I don't know why they included it with the other items."

"Let me take a look at that." Mitch picked up the paper then leaned over to the table next to them grabbing a paper cocktail napkin. He drew some lines—some straight, some curvy, some with points in the center. Looking back at Melanie's drawing, he then added a few Xs where the drawing had several short perpendicular lines, almost like telephone poles with mountains behind. Finished, he leaned back studying his sketch on the napkin. He erased one of the Xs and placed another one an inch higher. Putting his pencil down, he looked at Melanie.

"What is it? What do you see?" she asked him.

"I think your father drew a map. See these points and then one much higher in the middle? I think it's a mountain range and the higher point could be Mt. McKinley. Say it is McKinley. Then, if I'm not mistaken the upright lines point to an area where a large vein of gold was found around the time you said your father might have worked in this region. It was also around that same time that a man named Barrington registered a quick claim. He's now a billionaire."

Melanie looked out the window. Night had fallen so she saw her reflection. "There's one other thing I haven't mentioned. My aunt was terrified of my father, thought he was no good and that something bad was going to happen. She felt my mother and father were hiding something but they never told her what. And, one more thing. In the box was an old worn suede pouch with a small nugget, a rough rock, with little gold specs, like it was just picked up from a pile of rubble—a nugget of gold?"

"Maybe the drawing is a map of sorts where he picked up that nugget." Mitch paid the bill while Melanie returned the quilt and the rest of her things, along with Mitch's drawing on the cocktail napkin, into her bag. Mitch drove back to the lodge but there was little conversation. Both were deep in thought over what they had shared over dinner. They also seemed to have a heightened awareness of the other's presence. Melanie, when he kissed her cheek, felt the electricity shoot through her body as never before.

Melanie, she thought. *Take it easy. You just met Dr. Mitch O'Reilly.*

~ ~ ~

A MAN sitting at the end of the bar, his back to Mitch and Melanie, had stared at the couple's reflection in the mirror behind the bar. When he asked Millie who the woman was with the doc, she just shrugged. "I don't know, other than I overheard her say she bought a house and flew up here from Florida."

Chapter 12

FRANKLIN BARRINGTON, seventy-five, loved his home in Anchorage. His father founded Barrington Mining Corporation in 1915. Barrington Jr. added to the family fortune with the discovery of a large vein of gold in 1957. At that time an ounce of gold was valued at $34.95.

With the addition of the gold strike to the family corporation, Franklin could do no wrong. In 1983, with the death of his father, he inherited the corporation and built his dream home with a southern view over Cook Inlet, and to the north, the Alaskan mountain range loomed forever covered with snow.

Franklin knew his fishing boat, equipped with radar, was safely stored at a local marina. He no longer ventured out to sea, but his son went fishing almost every day in the summer months and kept the freezer full of salmon. His caretaker, Henry, had previously brought the floating dock in for the winter.

At four o'clock every afternoon without fail, Franklin, now the patriarch of the family, began his cocktail hour. He always dressed for the occasion—dark-red-velvet smoking jacket, three-carat diamond ring, and a heavy gold chain around his neck. Italian black-leather shoes beneath black wool trousers carried his muscular frame. His black hair had turned to silver around his temples. Seven years ago he saw a picture of a New York mafia don with slicked back hair. He liked the look and from then on applied a fresh amount of jell on his locks in the morning and again for the cocktail hour, or hours.

Sitting in the solarium—a floor to ceiling glassed in room overlooking the water, he waited for his son, Derek, to return from his visit to their corporate headquarters in Palmer. Franklin rang a little gold bell on the table beside his chair.

Cook, she had a name but was always referred to as Cook, bustled in with some canapés. She placed the tray on the coffee table and left the room. For some reason, Franklin was reminded of his late wife—a timid soul, rarely talked. Died one day without saying a word.

Cook inherited her mother's large Eskimo bones and her father's six-foot height. She had grown up in Juneau and worked as a sous-chef for a local hotel. Barrington, enjoying a particularly tasty salmon dinner one evening had asked to meet the chef. Fearing a complaint, the chef sent out the sous-chef. The woman, wringing her hands in a towel tucked in the belt of her white chef's coat, approached the table. After talking with the woman briefly, who said she learned to prepare game from her father who was a trapper, Barrington offered her a job at his home. Not hesitating a second, she accepted his offer.

The chance encounter was eight years ago and they both remained pleased with their decision. Franklin was continually enticed by his friends to ask Cook how to prepare moose, caribou, and the Alaskan's favorite fish, salmon. Thus Cook became another feather in Franklin's cap. Truth be told, Cook was especially pleased with the arrangement which gave her, along with room and board, more leisure time than the hectic, stress-filled hotel kitchen.

Franklin reached for a smoked-salmon crostini on cream cheese garnished with a sprig of dill. Taking a bite he savored the blend of flavors. He never over indulged at mealtime— watched his weight, and diligently worked out in the gym which he designed when he built the house. He had no cholesterol problems or any other malady for that matter.

"Cook, I'm home," Derek called out. "Fix my drink will you? I'll be in with father."

Franklin waited for his only child to join him, a smile crossing his face. He enjoyed Derek's company and especially the tall tales he related of his adventures at the mine, on the seas, hunting, and of the women. Ah, yes the women. "A chip off the old block that son of mine," he was known to say.

"Here you are, you old fox. How was your day?" Derek gave his father a soft punch on his shoulder—his sign of affection, his only sign of affection. He flopped down in his black-leather Eames chair across from Franklin and helped himself to a shrimp and tarragon crostini. "I'm starved. Oh, thanks, Cook."

"When will dinner be ready?" Franklin asked.

"An hour, unless you'd like it otherwise." Cook stood a moment waiting for his answer.

"An hour will be fine. Here, can you freshen my drink?" Franklin handed his glass to her and helped himself to a few cashews.

"Now, Derek, tell me about your day. Was everything in order at the office? No one pocketing any of those beautiful gold nuggets were they?"

"Well, I didn't rub elbows with any of the miners, if that's what you're asking. I did go over the books and checked on the shipments. But enough of that, I do have some interesting news."

Cook returned with Franklin's drink and then left to finish dinner preparations.

"So, what is this news," Franklin asked.

"When I left the office I took a run over to Houston and stopped at the bar."

"That's nice. See anybody I know?" Franklin asked taking a sip of his scotch.

"That's the news. Doc O'Reilly was there having a drink with a woman."

"Well, that is news. It's been several years since I've seen the doc with a woman. Was she pretty? How old?"

"Yes, she was pretty, blonde, and about my age—late thirties I guess. But there's more." Derek picked up the last crostini and took a bite. "I sat at the end of the bar not far from that window table. You remember that don't you?"

"Yes, yes, had many a song fest with my coal-miner friends after a day in the mine. Go on."

"Well, they were talking and joking around, I guess, but I heard him address her as Miss Beckett. I perked up when I heard the name because I remembered you telling me about a

Beckett—he and another man you mentioned in your stories of fifty years ago. I was only a twinkle in your eye."

Franklin straightened up in his chair. Staring at Derek, he asked, "What did they talk about?"

"I don't know. The only time they spoke up was that exchange of words when they were laughing. The rest of the time they seemed deep in conversation. Except she had this big purse—a tote I think women call it. She kept pulling stuff out of it—a picture, another piece of paper, and oh, yeah, a blanket. A quilt of some kind."

"Seems like they knew each other."

"Maybe, but then doc did a strange thing. He made a drawing of some kind on a napkin. I didn't see what it was. Directions of some kind for all I know." Derek finished his drink and stood up. "Cook just called us to dinner. Let's crack one of those new bottles of wine you ordered."

"All right ... I think I'll drop in on doc. See how his patients are doing. I read somewhere about a new treatment for black lung disease. Yes, I'll drop in and see what he's up to."

Chapter 13

BITS OF ICE pelted the window. The temperature had dropped suddenly as a fast-moving front slid into the area. Melanie scrunched down under the covers but sleep was elusive. Tossing and turning she felt frustrated with the lack of information in the search for her father. Houston had been a dead end.

"Come on, Melanie," she whispered. "You've only been in Alaska two days. Yeah, but it seems like a week. What did you expect—fly in and say, oh, hello, dad? Stop going over what didn't happen and make plans for tomorrow." She punched her pillow, lifted up on her elbow, and took a peek at the clock. It was nearly midnight. *A glass of hot milk, that's what I need,* she thought. *Yeah, that'll do it.* She hadn't asked Cathy about the bed and breakfast
    kitchen privileges, but she had to do something.

A fluffy white terrycloth robe was hanging on the inside of the bathroom door. An amenity Melanie quickly took advantage of, slipping it on over her navy-blue-flannel PJs. Forgetting to pack slippers, she pulled on a pair of the heavy socks that Mitch had insisted she buy and then pushed her feet inside the fringed mukluks, a heavy slipper-like boot, he had picked out for her. Glancing in the mirror as she left the room, she thought she looked like a blimp with all the bulky clothing, but she was toasty and that was all that mattered at the moment. She wasn't sure she could ever live in Alaska—so cold and it was only November.

Descending the stairs, lit top and bottom with nightlights, she plodded through the dining room to the kitchen as quietly as she could given her heavy footwear, and noticed a glow under the door. *Somebody else can't sleep,* she thought as she gently pushed the swinging door open. Mitch was sitting at the table twiddling a pen in his fingers over a small yellow pad in front of him. Hearing the door open he looked up and smiled at her.

"Cold are you? What are you going to do when the big snowstorms get here?" He laughed motioning for her to join him at the table.

"I couldn't sleep, and no, I'm not cold, at least not as long as I can pull on this bathrobe," she replied chuckling as she wrapped her arms around herself. "Do you think Cathy would mind if I warmed up some milk?"

"Not in the least. Can you heat up enough for two? I can't sleep either."

Melanie nodded she would. She found a small pan, two mugs, and pulled a half-gallon of milk from the refrigerator.

"Oh, oh, she cooks with gas. If I blow us up, it's been nice knowing you."

The kitchen was large—all pine: paneled walls, cupboards, and the kitchen table where Mitch was sitting on a pine captain's chair. He hadn't turned on the fluorescent light fixture over the island counter, opting instead for the smaller Tiffany-style hanging lamp over the table. Its soft glow gave just enough shadowy light for Melanie to see what she was doing over at the stove.

"I'm making a list of things I have to do in the next couple of days," Mitch said. "Sorry you can't sleep but I'm glad you came down. I'll show you what I've come up with, seeing how some of it pertains to a certain girl from Florida."

"Florida … seems a million miles away. Here's your milk. If Cathy comes down, she'll think we're a couple of old fogies sipping warm milk in the middle of the night." Melanie set his mug down and took a seat next to him.

"Or, maybe an old married couple content with each other's habits," he said, writing more notes on his pad. "Here, let me tell you what I've written down. Cheers." He raised his mug to her and tested the temperature of the milk with a small sip. "Perfect. Today … it is after midnight," he said, looking up with a grin on his face, his brown eyes dancing in the light. "I have to see a few patients, and, besides, the weather isn't that great for flying—"

"Flying?"

"Yeah. I've been putting off going to Cordova but it's on your list from the Interior Department. I'm not sure why the person you spoke with suggested Cordova. Kennecott Copper had several big mining operations around there but the company started closing the mines in 1929 and the last one closed in 1938, The Mother Lode. However, there is a very active historical society, and they give tours in the town of Kennecott. You should see the place—all the buildings are painted red because it was the cheapest paint at the time. It's possible they have access to employee records but it would still be prior to when your father was a miner. Maybe the guy thought someone in Cordova could come up with additional mines that were still operating in the late fifties. Anyway, we can take my bush plane—a nice little Piper Cub. It's not really mine. I rent it. But, the owner says I use it so much it might as well be mine."

"So you're telling me *you* are going to fly this, this little plane to Cordova?"

"Yes ma'am. There are lots of pilots up here. The distance between one place and another is so vast that it's the quickest way to get around. I have a bushman I see once every three months. He's about fifty miles from the nearest town but only accessible by water, dog sled, or a bush plane—really out in the wilderness. There's a river that runs by his place so in the summer he can navigate in a little boat to pick up supplies. But me, I take a sled team when there's snow on the ground and otherwise I fly planes equipped with floats—landing is always a little tricky. I've spent Christmas with him for the past four years."

"Will you go to see him this Christmas?"

"That's my plan. Anyway, after I take care of the immediate stuff today, I can fly us to Cordova tomorrow. I'll give you a couple of contacts to add to your list so you can set up some appointments and give them an idea of what you're looking for. How does that sound?"

"Mitch, it sounds too good to be true, but I can't let you rearrange your schedule like this. There must be a train or something."

"Cordova is only accessible by air and water. There used to be a bridge but it was taken out in the 1964 earthquake. You probably heard about it. It was awful and made all the papers—even those in the lower 48." He grinned.

"You have to let me pay you."

"Hey, I'm going anyway. Besides it would be nice to have some company, unless you don't want to fly ... with me ... in a little plane." He leaned back in his chair, cocked his head and raised his eyebrows.

"No, I wouldn't be afraid ... well, maybe a little," she answered furrowing her brow.

"Okay, then. You make your appointments. I'll see my patients and make sure the plane is ready. As long as we're in that area, let's take an extra day and hit the third town on your list, Kuskuluna Copper Center—if the people at Cordova think it would be worthwhile, otherwise we'll head back in the morning. That mine was part of the Kennecott operation so it's closed, too."

"Do you want me to make motel reservations?"

"No, we won't need a reservation, not at this time of year. We won't have any trouble coming up with a couple of rooms," Mitch said, finishing off his milk.

"Thanks a lot. Now I'll never go back to sleep. I need another mug of milk." Melanie stood and plodded to the sink.

"Can you make that two?"

She turned and smiled at him, shaking her head up and down. Suddenly the swinging door opened and Cathy popped her head in.

"Oh, it's you two. I thought I heard some talking. Warm milk, huh? Melanie, there's some instant cocoa mix in the cupboard next to the fridge if you want. Night." The door swung shut.

"I guess we've been discovered," Mitch said.

"She seems to know you quite well. Do you come here often?" Melanie asked, turning up the flame on the stove's burner.

"A few years ago I brought a woman with me when I was visiting a couple of patients in Sutton and then on to Chickaloon, two towns east of here. I always stay here when I'm in the area. Easier than driving back and forth from Anchorage."

"Ah, a woman. I was under the impression you weren't interested in the ladies. You haven't mentioned anyone." Melanie set their mugs on the table and sat in her chair snuggling with her knees pulled up to her chest, mukluks hanging over the edge, and taking a sip of milk. She looked at him waiting for his reply to her question.

"I lived with a woman for about three years, or rather she lived with me in my condo in Anchorage not far from my main office. But we decided to go our separate ways. She was a society type. Wanted to go to all the cultural events—concerts, museums, art galleries, fancy restaurants. With my work, I was beat at the end of the day, and emergencies always seemed to crop up on the weekends. It wasn't her fault. It was just that our routines and likes didn't mesh. How about you, Melanie? Ever been married?"

"No. Never married. But I have, or had, a long-term relationship—over four years. I didn't move in with him. I often wondered why not ... maybe because he didn't ask me, although it was assumed that one day we would probably get married. Actually, we just broke up."

Mitch leaned forward cradling his milk in front of him, intent on listening to what she was telling him.

"It all came crashing down when I bought my house and found the box, the box with the quilt and the drawing you saw. Alan didn't understand why I wanted to buy the house in the first place. Annoyed really, that I had made the decision without talking to him first, and just because the house was in the photo of my parents. Wasn't part of his plan for us. He said I was suddenly unpredictable." Melanie took a sip of milk reflecting on that last scene with Alan. "I had plenty of time to mull over our last conversation on the flight up here. I think I've become a different person … almost overnight. But when people hide your past from you and you suddenly start finding out about your parents … I wanted to learn more. I suppose I've become obsessed. Do you think I'm becoming neurotic, Doctor?"

"No," Mitch said, taking her hand. "A little crazy, maybe, but not neurotic. Now, it's time we try to get some shut eye." He picked up her mug with his and put them in the sink.

Melanie stood up and stretched. "You're right. Will I see you in the morning at breakfast or will you be leaving early?"

"I'll be long gone before you have your first cup of coffee, but I'll be back for dinner and then we can finalize our plans. I'll leave the names and numbers under your door of some Cordova people you can contact." Mitch put his arms around her in a bear hug and then took her hand, leading her to the stairs. "It's going to be a fun trip. I just hope it results in some information about your father." He kissed her hand, let it go and headed down the hall.

She watched him disappear into his room and went into hers. Snuggling under the covers, warmed by the hot milk and Mitch's hug, she was soon fast asleep.

Chapter 14

Anchorage, Alaska

DR. O'REILLY'S waiting room was packed. The light snowfall during the night did not deter his patients from keeping their appointments. He rented his office space in a medical building located at the edge of the Anchorage business district. The ground floor office insured easy access for patients with ambulatory issues. Pale-orange walls, the color of the sun's first morning rays, provided a cheery, warm atmosphere.

The outer door opened ushering in a puff of fresh air with a man. The gentleman, wearing a black-and tan-striped muffler, tan parka, and heavy boots under his black-wool trousers, doffed his hat. He approached the sign-in window breathing in the faint scent of alcohol.

"Hello, Carrie. I see the doc has a full house."

"Hi, Mr. Barrington. What can we do for you?"

"I was wondering if I could see him for a minute. Squeeze me in?" Franklin whispered. "My lumbago kicked up again. I thought it would go away with a few nights' rest, but it's getting worse."

"If you could grab a cup of coffee down at the café, I think I can *squeeze* you in—about thirty minutes. How does that sound?"

"Like a plan. Can I bring you a cup?"

"Two sugars, black," she replied in a hushed voice and a wink.

~ ~ ~

SITTING UP on the examination table, Franklin took another deep breath as Mitch moved his stethoscope along his back.

"Your lungs are good as ever," Mitch said. "Now let's see about that sore spot. Tell me when I hit it." He poked around Franklin's lower back. When he winced, Mitch continued to probe around the area. Pulling Franklin's flannel shirt down, Mitch turned to the computer terminal and scanned Barrington's record. "The last time you came in was three months ago." Mitch looked up at Franklin quizzically.

"My prescription ran out. I was hoping you could call it in again."

"No problem. Anything else bothering you?"

"No, no. Seem to be fit as a fiddle as they say. Derek told me he saw you the other day … with a lady." Franklin chuckled as he watched Mitch type in the script and send it on to his pharmacy. *Wonderful thing, technology,* he thought.

"Now don't go building igloos out of water, Franklin," Mitch said looking up over his reading glasses at the older man. "I bumped into her at the Eagles Nest Lodge. She's from Florida. Seems her father disappeared years ago and she's trying to find him."

"What's her name?"

"Melanie Beckett. You know what? You might be able to help. Can you, or Derek, look up an Arthur Beckett in your employee records? He might have worked at one of your mines back in the seventies. If you find anything, give me a call. I have to fly down to Cordova tomorrow to see some patients and Miss Beckett is going with me. She's making some appointments with the people at the historical society who handle the copper mine archives to see if they have any record of him."

"Well, yes. I'll call our personnel office. That's quite a ways back … not sure how good our records were then. Thanks for your time, doc. Have a safe trip to Cordova—you and the lady." Franklin chuckled again as the two men shook hands.

~ ~ ~

COOK PLACED a large bowl of her special New Orleans' recipe— jambalaya with Andouille sausage, and shrimp—on the dinner table. A bottle of Derek's favorite Chianti was open allowing it to breathe. In the summer, the two men preferred to dine in the solarium, but once the cold weather moved in they enjoyed the warmth of the dining room with a view of the fireplace through the archway leading into the living room. Derek didn't sit at the opposite end of the long mahogany table. He sat to the right of his father. Twin chandeliers positioned over the table were set on low with a dimmer switch, causing the multi-faceted crystals hanging from the branches to sparkle. Cook lit the candles on the table, three long-white tapers, giving an intimate feeling to the spacious room. The walls were lined with original oils of the spectacular Alaskan mountains depicted in various seasons of dress.

"I saw the doc today," Franklin said, buttering a piece of sourdough bread.

Derek poured some wine into his father's goblet and then his own. "What did he have to say about the pretty lady?"

"You were right. Her name is Melanie Beckett and she's from Florida." Franklin mopped up some spicy tomato sauce with a chunk of bread.

"Did you find out why she's here?" Derek asked taking a sip of wine. He looked over the rim of the glass at his father, scrutinizing his body language.

Franklin didn't face his son. "Seems her father disappeared. Doc is flying her to Cordova tomorrow to check the records at the historical society. She thinks he was a miner of some sort. He also asked me to check our employment records around 1950. See if Arthur Beckett is listed will you?"

"Do you think I'll find him ... in the records?"

"No. I'm sure not. Artie Beckett, Tommy Barnes, and I worked in the coal mine in Houston around then. Tommy died and Artie disappeared ... after that happened is when I found the gold and registered the claim with my father's company. That claim was the beginning of the gold division for Barrington Mining Corporation."

"So, you're telling me that is the only tie you have with Arthur Beckett—a coal mining buddy."

"That's what I'm telling you."

"Did you mention to doc that you once knew Beckett?"

"No. It was such a long time ago." Franklin picked up the little silver bell beside one of the candles and gently rang it once.

Cook bustled in. "Can I get you something, Mr. Barrington?"

"Yes. Will you bring me a scotch. No dessert tonight."

"And, can I get you something else, Derek," Cook asked turning to him.

"A cup of coffee would be nice. I'll take it in my study," Derek replied.

The two men didn't engage in further conversation. Franklin took his drink into the living room, ostensibly to watch the news on television.

Derek went to his study shutting the door behind him. The room was warm. The caretaker had ignited the gas fire—the usual winter routine in Derek's study. He found the long winter nights a bit depressing and looked forward to a little downtime after dinner, in his study, away from his father. Truth be told, Derek would not be sorry when the day came that he, Derek Barrington, would have complete control of the corporation. In the meantime, he was enjoying life without the stress of total responsibility for the various operations—daily decisions came easily to him. His father still handled the long-range, strategic planning.

The old man is hiding something, Derek thought. He never looked me in the eye when he talked about Beckett and Barnes. I've seen the articles on Tommy's death. Tragic and a little suspicious were words used in the newspaper account. Yet … nothing further was ever done about either man, he mused.

Derek put his coffee cup on the table beside the door for Cook. He had only taken a sip. The heavy, dark-green drapes were drawn across the expansive windows, and the low fire continued to burn in the gas grate. Derek stepped to the wet bar and poured himself a snifter of brandy. Returning to his recliner, he sat again in front of the fire, staring. "Cordova. I think I'll take a quick trip tomorrow."

Chapter 15

Palmer, Alaska

THE AROMA of fresh coffee, biscuits, and bacon and eggs wafted under the door of Melanie's room. Eager to see if Mitch had returned after she went to bed the night before, she quickly pulled on her new flannel-lined jeans, and navy-blue sweater over a white turtleneck shirt. She left the mukluks under the bed but did stick her feet into two pairs of heavy socks.

Trotting down the steps she saw Cathy talking to Mitch in the dining room. It was still dark at 8:30 but the fireplace provided an inviting glow to the room. Cathy looked up, greeted Melanie, and returned to the kitchen.

"Hey, sleepy head," Mitch said, giving Melanie a quick hug. "I was just contemplating whether to wake you or not. I stopped at the Palmer Airport yesterday and our plane will be ready and waiting for us. Did you line up a contact in Cordova?"

"Yes, a man—he'll be ready and waiting for me," she replied mimicking Mitch's words.

"Okay, then let's grab some breakfast and we'll be on our way."

~ ~ ~

MITCH GAVE Melanie a hand up into the Piper Super Cub plane and then immediately revved the engine checking the small control panel. The sun was bright but didn't seem to warm the seventeen-degree air.

"Are you sure this little toy can fly?" Melanie asked apprehensively, strapping herself into her seat in the cockpit.

"Fly? My dear, this baby can take us places in the bush no other flying machine would dare to go ... except maybe a helicopter."

"I will say it's cute, but I'll save other descriptive words for when I'm safely back on Mother Earth," she said in a loud voice in order to be heard over the noise of the engine and the whirling of the single propeller.

"Did you bring your sunglasses?" Mitch asked, putting on his pair that wrapped over his temples.

Melanie pulled hers out of the pocket in her red parka, put them on, then grinned over at the pilot.

"Okay, hang on … here we go."

The noise in the cockpit increased with the acceleration of the plane as it taxied down the runway picking up speed. They were quickly airborne.

"Whoa, that was fast," Melanie said wide eyed.

"That's what we bush pilots need—we usually have very little room to take off … or land. She cruises between ninety and a hundred miles-per-hour. This little bird is an 'Alaska Mod.' In other words she's been modified for Alaska, like the cold—feel that powerful heater?"

Melanie nodded pretending to wipe the sweat from her brow.

"Also a little more insulation so we don't have to shout. You, all right?"

"Yes. It's beautiful up here … the mountains … I can touch them. That Mount McKinley?"

"Yeah." He looked over at Melanie. "You'll get used to the noise."

She nodded, already able to hear better but still speaking a little louder than normal. "How long before we land?"

"About an hour," he said patting her hand. Mitch pulled back on the throttle of the Piper Cub. Responding to his touch, the little yellow bird rose higher streaking through a wispy white cloud.

"You're in for a real treat. Wait till you see the B&B I've booked for tonight. You won't believe it. But first we land at the Mudhole Smith Airport."

"Please tell me it's not really a mud hole."

"No, it's not a mud hole, but the Rose Lodge is on a barge with its own lighthouse."

"Quaint." Melanie let go of the handle on the side of her seat and leaned closer to the window.

"Cordova is on the east side of Prince William Sound—same area that was affected by the Exxon Valdez oil spill in March of 89. Commercial fishing, best salmon you ever ate, is the main industry."

"How many people live there? Hey, how about a cup of coffee. Cathy fixed a thermos for us."

"Love a cup. In 2008 the population was in the neighborhood of 2200. Cordova is a beautiful little city rising up on the slopes of a mountain from the water."

She handed Mitch a cup of steamy coffee. Sipping her own cup, she glanced out the side window. The view was beautiful—the ground below blanketed with snow, mountains piercing the heavens in the distance. She was enjoying the slightly bumpy ride and stole a sideways glance at her pilot. "You said you'd tell me about your practice."

"My practice. I specialize in respiratory ailments. But, while the population isn't huge, the ailments are varied so I'm more of a general practitioner. Then you add the great distances between towns, and even greater distances to help the bush people, a doctor gets hit with everything from the flu, to assisting women giving birth, to setting bones and then, of course, there's the black lung disease. Coal mining is a big part of Alaska's history. Unfortunately along with coal mining comes coal dust—although new ventilation systems have proven to be helpful. Somewhat."

"I've heard about black lung. Do miners still die from it?"

"Many of the old timers do. They were mining before the improvements, but there are still some of them around. The simple definition of black lung is that it's a chronic occupational lung disease contracted by the prolonged breathing of coal mine dust. *A simple definition.*" Mitch smacked his head at the word simple for such a painful existence. "It's also known as anthracosis, but my favorite is black spittle—a perfect, straightforward, *simple* definition. Black lung is anything but simple. No cure. Treatment is aimed at the symptoms and various complications like enlargement or strain on the heart which can lead to heart failure. The only real prevention is to take up another line of work."

Melanie saw Mitch's frustration as his body became rigid, his lips closed tight, and even despair in his eyes at not being able to cure his patients suffering with black lung.

"What are the signs? How does a miner know he's in trouble?" she asked.

"Oh, the symptoms are subtle at first—a slight cough. Then after a few years the cough gets nasty—spitting up a black inky substance. Once the dust is in his lungs, we can't get it out— kinda like a long-term smoker but worse."

"Can you detect it before the cough?"

"Yeah. Even if I don't see any signs, I always put a miner through a series of tests—chest X-rays and his pulmonary function. It usually affects miners over fifty. Heck, some of them start working in the mine as young as ten—family has to be able to buy food and clothes, so the males are in the mines from one generation to the next."

"So there's nothing that can be done?"

"Well, first of all a miner should use a respirator and not smoke. It's really sad to hear about coal workers experimenting with all kinds of self-medication. The traditional ritual of drinking a shot of whiskey with a beer chaser after a day in the mine supposedly brought up dust out of the throat. I also heard of the miners drinking morning bitters, to stimulate the coughing up of dust. Get this, they made a concoction of whiskey, snakeroot, gold seal and calamus root, sweetened with rock candy."

"Sounds awful. But I guess if you're desperate—"

"The number of miners being diagnosed with black lung is declining but the reports are misleading because of automation in extracting the coal from the ground. The percentage of workers contracting black lung is about the same."

Mitch looked out his side window and then at Melanie. "So many of these guys live in out-of-the-way places—like Clarence, my bush patient. I see most of these guys pro bono. There are a few rehabilitation centers that are trying to help."

"Want some more coffee?"

"Ah, yes. That's my dream—open a rehab center, maybe in Wasilla, or Palmer, or Healy. There's a big coal-mining operation now in Healy. A clinic that would be easy to get to—not in Anchorage—too congested."

"If there's no cure, what would you offer at a rehab clinic?"

"The same things that we all should do, but with black lung it's crucial. Exercise equipment, nutrition counseling, managing their disease, educating them on what the disease is and what they can do to help, and, of course, emotional support. In the late sixties, the government finally came up with workplace standards and a compensation package for miners with black lung, along the lines of the asbestos laws."

"Mitch, that sounds exciting and those who can't travel to you ... well, you've got Woodstock here," Melanie said, a smile spreading across her face.

"Woodstock. That's a terrific name for this yellow bird ... maybe I should buy her," he said returning her smile and taking another sip of coffee.

"When you said there's a chance your dad worked in the coal mines, and that he disappeared, my initial thought was that he could have been one of those who died from the disease." Mitch once again touched Melanie's hand. Picked it up and lightly kissed the creamy skin. "But we have no indication of that so let's not borrow trouble."

His kiss caused flutters in her stomach. She looked at him, wondering what to think of his warm advances, or was it just his kind bedside manner. Whatever, she looked forward to finding out.

"I know there's a possibility that he's dead, but my intuition tells me otherwise," she said. The plane bounced and she grabbed the handle above her window.

~ ~ ~

IN THE TERMINAL, Mitch gave the attendant instructions about his plane and then guided Melanie to the entrance. He flagged a cab and gave the driver directions to the museum where Melanie was meeting someone from the historical society.

"The driver will drop us off at the museum. I can walk from there to the office I share with another doctor when I'm here in Cordova. Here's his number. As we did before, whoever finishes first can call the other, and we'll set a time and place to rendezvous."

"What about the Rose Lodge—should we check in. I certainly wouldn't want someone else to take our reservation … on the barge."

"Not to worry," he said again kissing her hand. "I'll take care of it."

She smiled back at him as he opened the door to the cab. *All right, Sir Lancelot,* she thought. *I don't know what all the hand kissing is about, but I do know I like it.*

Chapter 16

Cordova, Alaska

THE DEICER crystals sprinkled on the walkway crunched under Melanie's feet. Per Mitch's instructions, she had worn her new boots. Her red parka's white fur lining around the hood framed her face. Each breath she exhaled looked like a puff of smoke escaping her mouth.

Pushing against the bar across the plate-glass door of the Cordova Museum's entrance with her gloved hand, she stepped inside and was greeted by the receptionist. She gave the young woman her name and told her she had an appointment with Walter Stein, the man in charge of the town's mining archives. Waiting, she strolled around the expansive lobby looking at the watercolor and oil paintings portraying life in Cordova over the years.

The receptionist called to her—Mr. Stein was ready to see her. Following the receptionist's directions, Melanie walked briskly down the hallway and rapped on the frame of the open door. Mr. Stein, forty something, black hair, and wearing a plaid flannel shirt tucked into chino trousers, rose from his chair and walked around his desk with his hand extended to Melanie.

"Miss Beckett, nice to meet you. Please have a seat. Would you like a cup of coffee?"

"Yes, please. I'm afraid it's taking me awhile to get used to your chilly, well, downright cold temperatures." Melanie was taller by at least an inch than the man standing in front of her.

Stein pressed a button on his telephone and asked to have two coffees brought in. As he talked into the receiver he sat down behind his desk and opened a manila folder lying in front of him. Scanning the top two sheets of paper in the folder, he glanced over at Melanie.

"After your call yesterday, I looked up your father's name, Arthur Beckett. I'm sorry to say we have no record of an Arthur Beckett working for Kennecott Copper. However, given the age you thought your father might have been, I'm not surprised as the mine closed in 1939."

"I see." Melanie's shoulders slumped, her eyes closing briefly.

"However, I'm pleased to tell you that I did find an Arthur Beckett, or rather a friend of mine found his name in his archives for the Jarvis Creek field in 1958. He worked there for the summer. Here's the phone number for my friend." He handed Melanie a slip of paper, stapled to a sheet with a typed list. "Your story intrigued me so I made up a list of various coal mines in the fifties through today in Alaska. Most of them operated for a few years and then closed, one after the other—strip mining operations. They're on that second piece of paper. That is all I have ... for the record."

A young boy entered the room with the coffees and left. Melanie's hand shook slightly as she pried back the top of one of the little containers and poured the cream into her coffee. Her pulse had jumped when he said that his friend had found her father's name. *Alice was right. Her father was a miner and had worked in Alaska.* Melanie blinked her eyes furiously, holding back tears. This man had just given her the first real piece of information, a concrete starting point—there was a record of Arthur Beckett. If only there was more information in that folder he was holding.

Taking a sip of the coffee, the cup cradled in both hands for warmth and attempting to stop her hands from shaking, she asked Stein if anybody around Cordova, or anyone connected to the mining operations in Alaska, might know her father. From the way he spoke, the hesitation when he added 'in our records' she felt he had something more to say.

"Not really, but there is a rumor ... you know how the old timers like to talk. It's part of the Alaskan lore, if you will. Have you heard of a Franklin Barrington?"

"Umm, not sure, who is he?"

"Well, Franklin Barrington, Sr., he's dead now, was the owner of one of the area's biggest coal mining operations around Anchorage—northwest of Palmer. His son, Franklin Barrington, Jr., worked in the mines. The old man wanted him to learn the business from the bottom up so Junior was required to work for a time underground, down the shafts, in various mining companies—shoveling the coal, wiring and setting the dynamite charges, loading the coal cars."

"Nice story, but what do the Barrington's have to do with my father?"

"I'm getting to that." Stein leaned forward over his desk and lowered his voice. "Franklin is said to have worked with your father, Arthur Beckett. In fact, he was buddy-buddy with two miners—your father and a Tommy Barnes. As the old timers tell it, the three went everywhere together. Inseparable. One day the three boys, they were barely twenty, took off on a week's breather from the coal dust and went prospecting. Again, the way the story is told, they found gold. At first they were just panning in a stream, but this later turned out to be a big gold strike."

"What did they do? Did they stake a claim?"

"Yes and no. The three started out for the claims office—at that time the closest one was in Anchorage. But, a big capital B U T, on the way Tommy Barnes turned up dead and your father disappeared. Junior registered the claim as part of his dad's mining company. Today the Barrington Mining Corporation is a billion-dollar operation—thanks to the gold."

"That sounds a bit strange," Melanie said, leaning forward in her chair to catch every word Stein was saying. "How did Tommy Barnes die?"

"Ah, now there the story changes depending on who's doing the telling. Some say he had a heart attack, but he was so young. The juiciest story has Junior killing Barnes, and that your father got scared and scampered down to the lower forty-eight somewhere." Stein leaned back. In a normal tone of voice, he said, "But the only verifiable information I have for you is that your father did work in the Jarvis Creek field for one summer."

~ ~ ~

NO SOONER had Melanie Beckett left Stein's office, then his phone rang. He recognized the voice.

"Walter, how are you?"

"Fine, Franklin. And you?" Stein asked.

"Oh, can't complain. My son, Derek—you remember Derek don't you?"

"Of course, Franklin."

"Last night at dinner he told me a cockamamie story about a Miss Beckett coming up from Florida ... looking for her father."

"A Miss Beckett?"

"Yes. You know that story that keeps floating around about when Artie, Tommy, and I found the gold?"

"Yes, sir."

"Well, if this Miss Beckett comes to see you ... asking about her father, I know that you wouldn't spread that nasty story."

"Oh no, sir. But she could hear the rumor from someone— you know, some old timers."

Chapter 17

MELANIE REMOVED her sunglasses as she entered the Crusty Salmon. She found the cafe cheerful, the sun's rays streaming in the picture window filtered slightly with lace curtains. Feeling a hand on her elbow she turned quickly and then smiled. Sir Lancelot had ridden up.

"Got your text message," Mitch said. "Do you mind sitting at the counter, the service is quicker. As you can see, this is the townies' fav place for lunch." Taking her smile as a yes, he steered her to the far end and two vacant barstools. "The fish sandwiches are great. What would you like to drink?"

"The sandwich sounds wonderful. Grilled. And, a cup of very hot tea with lemon, if they have it."

"You sound skeptical—we have lemons up here."

A young counter-girl, decked out in a frilly white apron covering a pink cotton dress, took their order.

"How did it go with Stein?" Mitch asked.

"Well, look who's here. Doc and a lady. This has to be a first."

"Derek, hello. The lady is Melanie Beckett." Mitch said. "Melanie, this is Derek Barrington."

Melanie's eyebrows shot up at the name. "Nice to meet you, Mr. Barrington." She nodded as their sandwich orders were placed in front of them.

"Sorry but we've had a run on lemons. We're out," miss pink dress said.

"No problem." Melanie laughed along with Mitch.

"You don't sound like you're from around here, Melanie. What brings you up north?" Derek asked.

Mitch looked down at his tea and then up at the mirror facing them. He watched Derek's reflection. Strange question, he thought. I saw his dad yesterday. I'm sure Franklin told Derek about my request to look up Melanie's father in their records.

"Actually, I'm on sort of a mission. I'm trying to find my father," Melanie replied taking a sip of the hot tea.

"Your father? What would he be doing this far from Florida?"

"What makes you think I'm from Florida?"

"I don't know—you sound southern and Florida's about as far south as you can get and still be in the U.S.," Derek said with an easy smile.

"My father left when I was a couple of months old. I'm trying to reconnect. A mutual friend of his said he was from Alaska, a coal miner. So I thought maybe he returned to his roots."

"Seems a stretch, but let me know if there's anything I can do to help. Gotta run. How long are you going to be staying?"

"As long as it takes," Melanie said.

"Maybe we'll bump into each other again. Bye, Doc."

Melanie cut her sandwich in quarters then laid her knife down. She continued to stare at her plate.

"What's the matter?" Mitch asked scrutinizing her in the mirror. Her brow was slightly furrowed—a polar bear could have sat down next to her and she wouldn't have noticed.

Melanie swiveled around slightly on the barstool and faced Mitch, her back to everyone in the cafe. "Walter Stein told me the most amazing story about Derek's father, Franklin Barrington." She paused and looked to Mitch for confirmation.

"Yes, Franklin is Derek's dad."

"Stein said that Franklin had worked with my father in the coal mines when they were in their twenties. And, just now Derek Barrington comes up to us in this cafe not an hour later. Have you heard the rumor about Barrington and two others finding gold, and that on their way to register the claim Tommy Barnes, that's the name Stein gave me, turns up dead and my father disappears. Have you heard that?"

Mitch picked up her hand, holding it in his. "Yes, I have. I didn't say anything yet because I wanted to see who told you the story."

"But why not tell me?" Melanie asked, jerking her hand from his. "That means you had heard of my father, knew his name."

"For one thing, the story has been around for years. I first heard it from a coal miner dying from black lung. I was just an intern at the time and these old guys can relate the darndest yarns."

"Mitch, I'm new here, but I'm not the new kid on the block. Are you holding anything else back from me?"

"No, except—"

"Except?"

"When you told me about your dad, when we ate at the restaurant in Houston, remember?"

"Of course, I remember. Go on."

"I couldn't help thinking about your dad with Tommy Barnes and Frankie Barrington. I started wondering if there was more truth than fiction to the story."

"Mitch." Melanie stood up, hands on her hips. "Stop talking in circles."

"Melanie, please sit down. Franklin Barrington is a very powerful man who runs a very powerful company who has a son who thinks he's powerful and will do almost anything to safeguard that power."

Melanie slid back onto the barstool never taking her eyes from Mitch's face, trying to understand what he was telling her.

"After lunch I'd like you to come with me to see two of my patients. They're both in their eighties. One has black lung and won't last much longer, and the other is as spry as they come. We'll tell them you're looking for Artie Beckett, and … well, we'll see what happens."

The two ate their sandwiches in silence. Mitch laid money for the check on the counter along with a generous tip.

Melanie drank the last of her tea, wiped her mouth gently with her napkin, and slipped her parka on. "I'm ready when you are," she said.

Chapter 18

MELANIE STARED out the cab window wrestling with her anger. Mitch's withholding the fact he knew of her father's name was inexcusable. Sir Lancelot had definitely fallen off his pedestal. Did he think she was an easy mark? No. He had been considerate and seemed interested in her search. Still he also kept secret that he knew about the rumor.

It was a little after three o'clock in the afternoon and the sun was dipping below the horizon. The miners lived at an assisted living home on the other edge of town. Within minutes the cab pulled to the curb and stopped. Melanie jumped out of the car while Mitch paid the fair. Inside he said a few words to the receptionist and then led Melanie down a wide hallway. They passed a woman in a wheelchair pushed by a nurse, and a visitor heading to the front door.

Two men, one bald the other with a fringe of white hair, were sitting across from each other at a card table, cards spread out in front of them. One of the men sat in a wheelchair. Another old-timer, his eyes closed, was listening to the television beside the gentle glow of the flames in the fireplace. Mitch and Melanie walked into the warm, cozy living room and over to the two men playing cards.

"How ya doing, Tony?" Mitch asked, shaking hands with the man in the wheelchair.

"Well, much better now that you bring us a pretty gal to look at."

"Tony, Sam, I'd like you to meet Melanie."

"Hi," Melanie said extending her hand to each of the gentlemen in turn.

"Melanie traveled here from Florida, and—"

"Florida? Now there's a nice place" Tony said. "Visited there once with my mother. She—"

"Nice?" Sam chimed in. "Must be God's country—no snow and no freezing your ass off. Sorry about the language,

Melanie, but I wish I was there right now. Maybe you can take me home with you—"

"Sam, for God's sake. Melanie's not going to take you home with her—doc maybe, but not an insufferable old grouch such as yourself." Tony laughed and immediately began to cough. Quickly pulling a handkerchief from his pocket he wiped something off his lips. Looked at the white cloth, then folded and returned it to his pocket.

Mitch pulled up two chairs and he and Melanie sat down.

"Hold on, you guys. Melanie is here to try to find her father," Mitch said.

"Father?" Tony asked. "What's his name?"

"Arthur Beckett. I have—" Melanie started to say.

"Artie Beckett?" Sam said looking over at Tony wide eyed, then turning back to Melanie. "Are you telling me that your Artie Beckett's daughter? Tony, doesn't that beat all? Old Artie must've married that pretty gal. You remember those pictures he showed us."

"Course I do. Now, there was a looker." Tony stared at Melanie, cocking his head one way then the other. "Yup, I see a resemblance. Don't you, Sam?"

"Sure do. But that gal of Artie's was just a kid. Such an age difference. We never took old Art seriously. He told us right off that there girl in the photo was the girl he was going to marry."

"What was it, ten, twelve years difference? Art was a baby himself—twenty-eight or so?" Tony said.

"I see we have guests," a matronly woman said joining the group.

"Hi, Martha," Mitch said standing. "I'd like you to meet Melanie Beckett. Melanie and I came here to visit these two grumps."

"Want a cup of coffee?" Martha asked, taking Melanie's hand.

Mitch looked at Melanie who nodded yes. "How about you guys?" he asked, turning to Tony and Sam.

"Oh, they're always up for a party," Martha said. "Be back in a jiffy. Mitch, can you help me? Couple of things I'd like to check with you."

The two walked off down the hall, Martha talking to Mitch in hushed tones.

"Tony, Sam, do you have any idea if my father is here … somewhere in Alaska?" Melanie asked. "I talked to a man, from the Interior Department, in Juneau. Not knowing where to start, I asked about mining communities. He gave me four, one being Cordova."

"No. No." Tony and Sam said in unison.

"Once he disappeared we never saw or heard from him again, did we, Tony?"

"That's right, but there were lots of stories," Tony said, coughing again.

Mitch returned with Martha. Glancing up at him, Melanie thought he looked upset, but she turned back to Tony and Sam. Martha placed a mug of coffee on the table in front of each person, the steam circling above. Melanie immediately grasped hers in both hands. Tony coughed again. Sam pulled his mug closer and looked at his friend, concern written on his face.

Tony coughed harder, gagging, unable to catch his breath. Mitch grabbed his bag and pulled out an inhaler and stepped quickly to Tony's side. Putting the inhaler over his mouth, Tony took a few quick breaths. Mitch removed the inhaler and bent the man over encouraging him to spit up what was caught in his throat. Tony fumbled for his handkerchief but Mitch already had a paper napkin under his mouth, catching the black goo that slowly spilled out over the man's lips.

As everyone watched, Tony began to breathe easier and then straightened up in his wheelchair. Mitch held the coffee cup to Tony's lips and encouraged him to take a swallow.

"Use this inhaler when you can't catch your breath. Sam, here's another one for you. I'll take a look at both of you in your room before I go. You okay, Tony?"

"Yeah, thanks. Melanie, you were about to ask us a question before I so rudely interrupted you."

"You just wanted her sympathy," Sam retorted, leaning back in his chair and egging on his friend. The concern now erased from his face.

"I was wondering if you could tell me about the stories?" Melanie asked looking from one man to the other. Mitch closed his bag and pushed back from the table, watching the scene play out between Melanie and his two patients.

"Well, the version I like," Sam said, "had Artie, Frankie Barrington, and Tommy—what was his last name? Tony, help me out here. Goldarned if I don't forget."

"Tommy Barnes."

"Yeah, that's it Tommy Barnes," Sam said. "Well, the three of them found some gold. But Frankie told his old man, Franklin. The old man up and registered the claim under the Barrington Mining Corporation. People say the three guys had a falling out on their way to the claim's office and that Artie took off with a hunk of gold never to be seen again."

"Honestly, Sam, that's not how it was at all," Tony said. "The boys did find the gold but Tommy Barnes had an accident—fell off a cliff. They found his body sometime later. The way I remember it, the three split off for some reason. Frankie went to his dad, Tommy ended up breaking his neck, and Artie, here I agree with you, was never seen again."

Chapter 19

Anchorage, Alaska

FRANKLIN, HIS NERVES a bit edgy, began his cocktail hour early. He was glad he had his little chat with Stein at the Cordova Museum, and he was glad Derek had not been home in time to join him in the first two drinks of the evening. Nerves now under control, Franklin responded to Cook's call that dinner was ready. He went directly to the dining room and helped himself to a bowl of moose stew. He loved to fish, but hunting had never been one of his favorite sports. Consequently friends, at the end of hunting season, always brought their excess kill to Franklin. Cook had a secret method in preparing game meat—her dishes were always tender and juicy, almost always.

Savoring his first bite of the stew, Franklin looked up hearing Derek enter the house.

"Dad," Derek called out. "I'm late—you have dinner?"

"Just started. Get yourself a drink and join me in the dining room," Franklin replied.

Derek's place was already set at the table when he joined his father and he immediately helped himself to the stew.

"Where've you been," Franklin asked. "No drink? Help yourself to the wine."

"Cordova Museum. Met with Stein. Do you want some more wine, Dad?" Derek asked, filling his own goblet.

Franklin nodded, yes, popping a morsel of meat into his mouth and closing his eyes to savor the taste. "Cook sure does know how to prepare moose. Did Stein have anything interesting to say?"

"No, we just chit-chatted. He mentioned he had had a busy couple of hours but other than that the museum had been quiet. I did spot doc going into the Crusty Salmon with Miss Beckett. I stopped to say hello and doc introduced me to her."

"What did you think of our Miss Beckett?"

"Not sure why you call her 'our Miss Beckett.' Nice enough, pretty, very intent on finding her father. Dad, I keep hearing stories, especially now that Melanie—"

"Melanie is it," Franklin chuckled leering at his son. The stories never ceased to amaze the elder Barrington about his son's exploits with women.

"Yeah, she is a looker, Dad, but don't change the subject. Tell me how you remember those days when you three guys found the vein of gold."

"Ah, Derek, do we have to dredge up the past?"

"I'd like to hear it again ... from you. After all, you ended up with the gold that established the new division of our company."

"Yes, and rightly so," Franklin said in a testy voice. "There's nothing mysterious about it. The three of us went prospecting—took a week off from the coal mine, and at first did some panning in Yellow Creek. When we realized that each of us had come up with a significant amount of gold from our efforts, we began to investigate the out-cropping nearby. We found an abandoned mine shaft—no more than a hole to crawl through and about fifteen feet long. The opening was covered with vines and partially blocked with rocks. We pulled away the debris so we could enter and found the beginning of a vein. Some miner before us probably tried to hide his find and died before he could stake his claim."

"Okay, but then what happened?" Derek poured himself some more wine as well as topping off his father's goblet.

"We headed back to Anchorage to register the strike but we got separated. I made camp that night—thought maybe Artie and Tommy would see the fire and join me. Then I got to thinking that maybe they didn't want to join me. Maybe they hustled ahead of me. Maybe they intended to stake the claim for themselves cutting me out. So, hell, I made a beeline the next day to my dad and we registered the claim as part of Barrington Mining Corporation."

"Did you ever see Tommy or Artie again?"

"No, and you know very well that Tommy's body was found—apparently at the bottom of a rock slide. Never did see or hear from Artie again. I assume after all these years he's either dead or doesn't want to be found."

~ ~ ~

THE NEXT MORNING Derek went to the Anchorage Daily News and asked to see the paper's archives starting in 1957. He was led to a cement-block room, much like a vault. There were a few gray-metal desks, war surplus, with gray metal folding chairs in various stages of disrepair. Each desk had a computer terminal and a microfiche reader. Microfilm was the only method to quickly scan the very old editions of the paper.

Because Tommy Barnes was linked to Franklin Barrington and hence to the Barrington Mining Corporation, Derek surmised that when they found Tommy's body the story would appear on the front page. He had only spent an hour bent over the fiche reader, advancing from paper to paper when he spotted the article. The story was short and to the point. Tommy Barnes' body was spotted by a bush plane in route to delivering the week's mail to various outlying towns. Cause of death was a fall as a result of a rock slide. The article stated that Barnes was survived by his parents who lived in Juneau.

Derek scanned another month of papers but did not come across any more articles. He leaned back in the chair, and feeling a chill pulled his parka around his shoulders. Staring at the last paper displayed on the fiche reader he went over what his father had told him the night before and began rolling around what-if scenarios in his mind. But every time he came back to his father's story, and Melanie's determination to find her father, he asked himself why?

Why is this woman so determined, and if she does find her father, what will his version of the story be? Could it be that, as Franklin said, Artie was trying to claim the gold find for himself? When Franklin's father claimed the find for his company, maybe Artie thought that somehow he could charge Franklin Barrington with claim jumping. What if Artie's daughter found him and together they sued the company for half of the gold fortune. What if Artie won the case? Life as I know it will be over.

Derek left the newspaper, drove to an isolated spot overlooking Cook Inlet and parked. Digging his cell phone from his pocket, he scanned the telephone numbers he had stored. Finding what he was looking for, he connected to the number.

The phone rang twice and then there was a click—someone had picked up.

"Sid, are you there?"

"Derek, nice to hear from you. What's up—you want to buy me that drink you owe me?"

"Maybe, but right now I have a job for you. I'm trying to find an old miner. His name is Arthur Beckett, about seventy-five. Rumor has it he could be in Alaska somewhere."

"Well, that certainly narrows down a search—in a state bigger than Texas."

"He worked with my father and a Tommy Barnes in some of the area's coal mining operations as a mucker around 1957. Sorry, that's all I have right now. If I get anything further I'll call you."

"A mucker?"

"Yeah. They are the miners down in the shafts who shovel the coal and mud into carts to be hauled up to the surface after setting off the dynamite charge."

"And what do you want me to do if I find this Artie person?"

"For right now, I just want to know where he is. However, he may have to disappear again. For good."

Chapter 20

AWKWARD SILENCES. The cab ride to the Rose Lodge after meeting with the two miners. Checking in. Then dinner. Neither Mitch or Melanie talked except for the perfunctory, "please pass the butter." Both retreated into their own thoughts.

Melanie excused herself from dinner, saying no to dessert or another glass of wine. She told Mitch it had been a long day and with all the information she had received, real or not, she had much to think about. She was tired. At his suggestion earlier in the day, she said she had made an appointment for the next day at the Sutton Library, twenty minutes east of Palmer. They agreed to meet in the dining room by ten o'clock in the morning to fly back to Palmer.

Melanie entered her room on the second floor of the lodge, and leaned back against the door. Her thoughts went immediately to Tony and Sam. Something happened at the miners' home. Mitch had suddenly withdrawn from her, the miners, and everyone around him.

She stepped to the window and looked out over the black water of Prince William Sound. The night was cold, a minus two degrees she had heard the waitress say to guests at another table, but the sky was clear. The moon was out reflecting off the water below. She pressed her forehead against the cold pane of glass still upset that Mitch hadn't told her about the rumor. There certainly had been several opportunities since they met.

Feeling a sudden chill, she turned away from the window and quickly changed into her flannel PJs, throwing her clothes on the chair. Snuggling under the heavy down quilt, she again ruminated over the day, tossing and turning in the king-size bed. Her spirits had soared when Stein came up with her father's name … and then there was the rumor … how coincidental it had been that Derek Barrington had walked into the café where she and Mitch were grabbing a quick lunch.

Then those two lovable characters, Tony and Sam, again relating the rumor of her father—each with their own variation of the story. However, in each case, Stein's and the two buddies at the home, the crux of the story was the same— three men, her father being one, had panned for gold. Her father disappearing. "That must have been the time when he came to Florida and ultimately married my mother," she whispered. "But he had met her before because Tony and Sam saw a picture of them and—"

Was someone at the door? She sprang from the bed. Stood still on the carpet—listening. There … a soft knock on the door. She padded closer, cocking her head.

"Mel," a man whispered.

She took another step. "Who is it?"

"Mel."

It was Mitch. She opened the door and he fell forward into her arms knocking her backward. He reeked of cigarette smoke and liquor. She struggled to regain her balance, holding him up so he didn't slither to the floor.

"Mel," he slurred. He looked up—his eyes full of pain, the same pain she had seen on his face earlier when he was talking about black lung. But this was far worse. His face was drawn with despair, tortured.

Tearing her eyes from his face, she dragged him away from the door.

"Come on, big guy. Let's get you onto the bed before you fall down."

He tried to move his legs but his ankles turned over causing him to stumble. Melanie guided him, and when he bumped into the edge of the bed he fell forward but then started to slide off. Melanie grabbed a leg and pulled his butt on top of the bed, then the other leg turning him on his back. She ran to the door, shut it, and then turned on the bedside lamp. The man prone on her bed had passed out.

She stood staring down at him. *Whatever happened today at the home is still with him,* she thought. *What could be so bad that he drank himself into this condition?*

"I guess you're not going to your own room tonight," she whispered. Leaning over the bed she took a closer look at his face. His eyebrows were drawn together and his forehead furrowed. "You may be passed out, but something terrible is going on in your mind. Okay, so, Melanie, what are you going to do? Well, first, I'll get those boots off."

Struggling to remove his heavy boots, she thought for sure he would wake up, but he didn't. She then pulled the quilt up around his shoulders, turned out the light, and crawled up under the blanket on the other side of the bed.

Shivering, or shaking from Mitch's sudden appearance, she wasn't sure which, her body finally became still under the warmth of the cover. She turned on her side and stared at the man who had befriended her and who had seemingly wanted to help her find her father.

His hand lying next to her was balled into a fist. Melanie laid her hand over his—his fingers slowly curled around hers and she fell into a light sleep.

"No! No! No!"

Melanie's eyes shot open. Mitch was crying out, again in distress. His hand gripped hers as his head shifted quickly from side to side, tears trickling down his rough skin to the stubble of his beard's new growth since his last shave.

Slowly, his body fell limp, his hand remaining in hers, but the grip had eased. Melanie closed her eyes and again slept. Mitch cried out again and he continued to moan, until he finally fell into a deep sleep.

Waking, Melanie glanced at the clock. It was 6:30. Looking at Mitch lying next to her, she saw his breathing was rhythmic and his body relaxed. She inched her way off the bed so as not to rouse him. Tiptoeing, she picked up her clothes off the chair and went into the bathroom, shutting the door softly behind her. Turning on the light over the mirror she looked at her haggard face. She decided to shower, get dressed, and then try to wake Mitch up.

Standing in the shower, she turned the water on as hot as she could stand it and let it sluice over her body. She slowly began to feel better—the bathroom now a steamy cocoon.

Stepping out of the shower she grabbed the fluffy white bath towel and briskly rubbed the soft cloth over her body. She was in no hurry to wake the man sleeping on her bed.

Who was he going to be—the tender man who kissed her hand, or the tortured man who fell into her arms last night?

Using the hairdryer wired beside the mirror, she blew her blonde strands into place and then dressed. She was ready. With one last look in the mirror, and a sigh, she slowly opened the door a crack … then pushed it open wide.

The bedside lamp was on and Mitch was gone. There was a note on her pillow: "I'll meet you at ten in the dining room for breakfast. Sorry about last night. Mitch"

A little before ten Melanie went downstairs, poured herself a cup of coffee at the service laid out at the entrance to the dining room and then went in. Mitch was sitting at a table on the far side of the room next to a window, a cup of coffee in one hand and a newspaper in the other. The window revealed the sun was up over the horizon—a brilliant sunshine-filled day. He looked up and saw Melanie in the doorway.

She couldn't read his face—he wasn't smiling, but he wasn't frowning either. He stood up as she walked over to him.

"Hi. How are you feeling?" she asked, a half smile playing on her lips.

"A little rough. Thanks for your help last night."

"Do you want to tell me what happened?"

"No … it won't happen again." His voice was just above a whisper. Soft.

"Sure you don't want to talk?"

"No. Not now. Sometime … maybe never."

She could barely catch his words. She wasn't sure she heard him correctly.

They finished breakfast in silence. With his third cup of coffee he looked up and forced a smile. "I called the airport. Woodstock is ready to go when you are. We'll fly to Palmer and drive to Sutton—you go to your appointment at the library and I'll see my patient. Then we'll drive back to Palmer."

Chapter 21

MELANIE WAS trying with all her might to forgive Mitch. How could he have held back the story, the rumors, the fact he had heard the Beckett name before. They had only spoken a few words to each other since her outburst in the café yesterday. And the Barrington name. Suddenly everyone she talked to mentioned Barrington in one context or another. And, he didn't explain why he showed up at her room, drunk, passing out on her bed. Was there something she could do … but, he'd have to let her.

Sighing, she glanced at Mitch as he banked the yellow bird for the approach to Palmer Airport. She knew he only had one patient to see while she visited the Sutton Library office.

Mitch taxied the plane to the parking area near the terminal and stopped. He didn't move, just stared out the side window turning away from Melanie.

"Mitch, it's okay if you don't want to tell me what happened yesterday. I don't mean to pry. But if you change your mind, I can be a pretty good listener." She put her hand on his sleeve.

He turned to look into her eyes, eyes filled with concern for him.

"Melanie, I appreciate your caring, but right now all I want to think about is how can I help you. I can't imagine how difficult it must be—thinking maybe, some way, somehow, you're going to find your father. What worries me is how you're going to feel if you find he's dead. I hope to God he's alive, but you have to prepare yourself."

"I know that's a possibility." Melanie looked down at her gloved hand. "But for now, let's plan on finding him alive. I'll have to accept the other if the time comes … but in my heart I think he's alive and out there … out there somewhere waiting for me. Okay?"

Mitch put a gentle hand on her neck pulling her head forward and softly kissed her lips. Leaning back, he smiled into her big blue eyes. "I'm with you. Now let's leave Woodstock to the care of its owner and get going to Sutton to see what we can turn up."

Mitch climbed out of the plane and walked around to help her down. Melanie couldn't move. His kiss was something new—so sweet, so tender—filled with the promise there would be more. A warmth flooded her body she hadn't felt before, melting away her anger. She wanted to learn more about this man—a friend, a doctor. He was hiding something from her, something terrible. But what? Perhaps he would become her lover? So many questions.

One thing was certain. The tension between them left with his embrace. She knew she cared about him, perhaps more than she wanted to admit, but for the first time in her life she wasn't afraid to let herself find out.

~ ~ ~

IN LESS THAN thirty minutes, Mitch pulled into the Sutton Public Library. The small building looked like a converted barn. Like most old wood buildings in and around mining towns in Alaska, it was painted red. He let Melanie out and then drove off to see his patient.

Entering the building, she saw the walls were lined with pine bookcases and inhaled the familiar library scent of rows and rows of shelves holding the books that would entertain, teach, and inform those who opened them. An old man was returning an armful of books to their proper place. He looked up, stared at Melanie for a moment, then turned and limped to another bookcase. Behind a wooden counter, worn smooth with age, was an open door marked Office. A woman, hearing the soft buzzer indicating someone had come into the building, stepped out to greet Melanie.

"You must be Melanie Beckett. I know most of our regulars," she said smiling.

"Yes, I am. Thank you for seeing me."

"My name is Peggy Eaton. I'm the Sutton-Alpine Librarian. How's that for a mouthful," she chuckled. "Come in and sit down. I was given the task of searching the mine's records for Arthur Beckett by the person you spoke with at the historical society here in town. Gus, can you come here a minute?"

The man Melanie had observed when she came in poked his head around the door.

"Can you get Miss Beckett and me a cup of coffee? The way she's rubbing her hands trying to get warm they'll soon be raw."

"Sure, Peggy." The man limped out the door.

Following Melanie's gaze, Margaret said, "Gus was caught in a mine cave-in years ago. Lost his left leg. He works here part time—at seventy-two he's sharp as a tack. The job keeps him in spending money."

Melanie turned back catching the compassion on Peggy's face as she scanned her computer screen. Gus reappeared with a small tray carrying two mugs, a few creamers, packets of sugar, napkins, and little red stirrers.

"Thanks, Gus," Peggy said.

"Don't you people ever get cold?" Melanie asked, picking up a mug and wrapping her fingers around it.

"Hey, this is nothing. Wait til winter really hits," Peggy said, picking up the other mug. "Cream, sugar?"

"Yes, please." Melanie helped herself to two of the creamers and smiled at Gus as he limped out of the office.

"Melanie, we've searched back to 1950 and the man, who looks after the records, and I didn't find a trace of an Arthur Beckett. Did someone tell you he had worked in one of the mines around here?"

"Not exactly. When I called the Department of the Interior in Juneau, they included Sutton, Houston, Chickaloon and Eska. I visited Houston and Cordova. My friend, Dr. O'Reilly, suggested I come here since I was so close—I'm staying in Palmer."

"So, Mitch is a friend of yours. Good man. He'll take care of you. But I don't think there is anything else I can do for you. If you come up with more information, where you think I might help, give me a call. Here's my card."

"Thank you, Peggy." Melanie drank the last drop of her coffee, closed her parka and shook hands with the librarian. Leaving the office she walked to the front entrance and pulled out her cell to call Mitch, letting him know she had completed her meeting. The sun was bright, so she stepped outside thinking it might be warm, after all, in Florida in the middle of winter, the sun is very warm even if it's below sixty degrees. Of course, in Sutton it was well below freezing.

She quickly thought better of her idea and returned to the warmth of the library. Setting her tote down on a table in the corner she picked up a book that had been left on the chair—*The History of Sutton*. She sat down and started leafing through the pages. Hearing uneven footsteps, Melanie looked up to see Gus limping toward her.

"Miss Beckett, mind if I sit with you while you wait for the doc?"

"Not at all. Peggy said you were a miner. I've been visiting several of the old mining towns trying to locate my father. I still have to visit the Usibelli coal mining company in Healy." Melanie looked off into space, blowing into her gloves to warm her nose. "It will probably be more of the same—never heard of Arthur Beckett, or maybe he worked there as a young man and then fell off the face of the earth."

"Melanie … mind if I call you Melanie?"

"Of course you can call me Melanie," she said bathing Gus with a smile as she patted his hand.

"Melanie, your father did return to Alaska after his wife died. But he changed his name."

"What? Gus, what are you saying?" she gasped.

"I worked in a mine with him—before I was hurt. One night after our shift, your dad and I went to the bar for a beer. We were both feeling a little low, very low, and I guess we had more than one bottle, actually we had several. But no matter how much Artie drank, he couldn't stop the agony that was haunting him. So, he'd have another drink. He told me he was afraid. Never said afraid of what. But he did say he was afraid to come back to working in the mines unless he changed his name."

Melanie's eyes filled with tears as Gus talked. Finally, a real connection. She wasn't crazy for coming to Alaska after all, trying to find her father.

"Gus, what's his new name?"

"Andy Bennett."

"Do you know where he is? Please, dear God, tell me you know where he is."

"No, no. That was almost thirty years ago. He'd be too old to go down in the mines now. Besides once I was hurt, we never saw each other again."

"Did he mention his baby, a baby daughter? Gus, did he say my name?"

"Yes, Melanie. But it was very painful for him. He told me that just before his wife died, they had a baby girl ... he said, 'Melanie was a beautiful baby.'"

Tears spilled downed Melanie's face. She looked into Gus's eyes, trying to see the man in his mind, the man he was speaking about, her father.

"He never mentioned his wife and baby again. I know he continued to hold you close to his heart ... you could see it in his eyes, a look we would exchange from time to time. But ... never again could he bring himself to say your name."

Melanie slowly put her arms around Gus's shoulders and kissed his cheek.

"Thank you, Gus. I have something to show you." Melanie opened her tote, and the zippered compartment with the picture.

"Look, Gus. Is this the man you just called Andy Bennett?"

"Yes. Believe it is. And the woman—he showed me her picture that night in the bar. Always kept it in his pocket I guess, but he never brought it out again. A course, he's changed—the mine does that to a man. Probably looks very different now. Is the baby you, Melanie?"

She dug down into the bottom of her tote and pulled out the little quilt. She placed it on the table next to Gus's hand. He ran his rough, gnarled fingers over the little squares … gazed at the picture … looked up at Melanie, a smile crossing his weathered face.

They both looked up at the sound of the buzzer. Mitch saw the two of them in the corner and sauntered over.

"Gus, how are you doing?"

"Just fine, doc. Me and this little lady have just had quite a chat."

Mitch saw the picture and the quilt lying side-by-side on the table. His eyebrows shot up as he turned to Melanie.

"Mitch, Gus has just told me an amazing story. He knew my father … they were friends after he disappeared. Mitch … he changed his name to Andy Bennett. No wonder no one can find his name."

"Gus, how long have you carried this secret," Mitch asked.

"Over forty years, I figure," Gus said.

Melanie returned the photo and the quilt to her tote and stood up to leave. "If I find him, Gus, I'll let you know."

"I'd like that, Melanie. I hope I've been of help. Take care."

Melanie kissed his cheek, wiped her eyes with the sleeve of her parka, and took a few steps to the front door that Mitch was holding open for her. She turned and looked at Gus again. He had followed her to the door. Giving him a hug, she thanked him again and watched him as he limped to a chair, picked up a couple of books and put them under his arm. He turned to her and each gave a tentative wave. Melanie pulled the library door shut and trotted to catch up with Mitch.

Chapter 22

FRANKLIN CHALKED his cue stick. Bending over the pool table he took careful aim, drew back his stick, and gently tapped the 6 ball into the corner pocket.

"Nice shot, Dad," Derek said. He took a sip of his second happy-hour martini.

"I've asked my secretary to make a list of possible guests for a Christmas party. Invitations won't go out for another two to three weeks," Franklin said watching his son chalk his stick.

"That's nice," Derek said, tapping the 4 ball. The ball slowly made its way across the green felt stopping on the edge of the center pocket. He took another sip of his drink. "Any particular reason? You haven't thrown a party for almost a year."

"Yes, as a matter of fact, I do have an ulterior motive. I want to meet the Beckett woman. See if she has her father's spunk."

"She's a looker, I'll say that for her." Derek snapped his cue into the wall cabinet. "I'm tired of playing. You're too sharp tonight."

"Something bothering you, Derek. You're not performing in your usual cutthroat manner," Franklin said his words dripping with sarcasm.

"No, not really. Hungry I guess."

The phone rang and Derek snapped up the receiver. "Hang on a minute. Dad, I'll meet you in the dining room. I've been waiting for this call. Won't take me long."

Franklin nodded to his son, returned his cue to the case and left the room.

"Okay, Sid, whatcha got?"

"Dr. O'Reilly flew Beckett to Cordova—"

"I know that. I talked to them in the cafe." Derek frowned, downing the remainder of his extra-dry martini.

"Yeah, I saw you. Then he flew her back to Palmer and they drove to the Sutton Library of all places and the doc left. She was in there quite a while and then the doc came to pick her up. He went in and about twenty minutes later he and Beckett came out. She turned in the doorway and kissed the cheek of an old guy. Then they drove away."

"I wonder what that means," Derek said, looking into the bottom of his empty glass.

"I went in the library and there the old guy was, standing by a bookshelf, just staring. I asked him a few questions about the operation on a pretext of doing a story for the Anchorage Daily News. I told him I saw him talking to a woman and did she work for the library. He said no, that she talked with the librarian, Peggy Eaton, after that she was waiting for her ride and they chatted. Beckett told him that she didn't get any information from the librarian. That she was just trying to find her father. He told her that he was sorry he couldn't help her either."

"That's it?"

"Yeah, but I'll keep on it … if you want me to."

"Yes, of course, I want you to. Franklin's throwing a Christmas party in a few weeks. I want you to come, as my guest, but I won't say anything to my dad. You just show up."

Chapter 23

MELANIE WAS riding an emotional rollercoaster. Low one minute angry enough to spit nails at Mitch, and now exhilarated after talking with Gus. Mitch was at the wheel, driving back to the Eagles Nest from Sutton. Melanie, sitting catty-corner to face him, the seatbelt straining against her shoulder, chattered non-stop. Her body language said it all—her father was so close she could almost reach out and touch him. Mitch, a smile on his face, never let go of Melanie's hand.

There was one thing that bothered her—the fact that Arthur Beckett was so afraid that he left his baby and he changed his name. He was afraid for his life. The question she'd carried with her over the years—why did her father leave her—was answered. He was afraid for her life as well.

Everything she'd been told seemed to point back to the time Frankie, Tommy, and her father found the gold. He had left the clue in the wooden box—the rock with flecks of gold. Her next step was to dig into the newspaper files. There must have been a story on Tommy Barnes' death, maybe even a mention of Arthur Beckett.

Mitch agreed. In the morning he said he'd drop her off at the Anchorage Daily News, go to his office to take care of his patients, and then meet her for lunch at a café near the Anchorage Museum of History and Art.

~ ~ ~

MELANIE SHIVERED as the attendant explained the microfiche storage system and the various methods Melanie could use to find the time period she was looking for in the vast archives. Time flew by the first two hours. She found an article describing how Tommy Barnes' body was found. Franklin Barrington told the police where he had last seen Tommy, but nothing else appeared the following days or months. She scanned back to the first article that was written about his death and then advanced slowly page by page through the newspapers for the following four months. An obscure article, second section, third page on the left-hand side, titled: "Barnes' Death an Accident?" caught her eye. It was only a couple of paragraphs, submitted by a Doris Hill. The gist of the piece was that Hill questioned whether Tommy's death was an accident. She wrote that the circumstances looked suspicious.

Melanie glanced at her watch. She had to hurry to meet Mitch. She tucked the printouts of the two articles she found in her purse. Holding her parka close to her body, and power walking down the sidewalk, she followed the directions Mitch had given her to the cafe. Stopping twice, she turned around feeling somebody was behind her … calling to her … or maybe following her. The frigid air made her nose run and she was happy to see the café and grateful to feel the warm air as she stepped inside. The café was bright, crisp white café curtains in the window, and very noisy from the clatter of dishes, jukebox music, and the patrons' animated chatter. Spotting Mitch at a table in the middle of the lunch crowd, she slid into the chair next to him.

"Hi," he said, rising to greet her. "Wrap your little hands around that mug of coffee."

"Thank you. Oh, that does feel good. Look what I found." Melanie slid her fingers into her purse and pulled out two sheets of paper. She handed them to Mitch and then quickly returned her fingers to the warm coffee mug.

"Suspicious?" Mitch looked up at her.

"How about that. I was running late so I didn't ask at the desk about this Doris Hill. She's probably long gone, but I'll try. See why she thought it *suspicious*."

"We've been invited to a Christmas party," Mitch said. "An invitation was waiting at my office along with a stack of messages. There was a hand-written note at the bottom of the invitation by none other than Franklin Barrington, specifically asking me to bring the visitor from Florida. That would be you." He smiled as the waitress placed two grilled-chicken wraps in front of them and then bustled off. "Sorry, but I ordered these. I knew our time would be short."

"Ah, Franklin Barrington. I want to meet that man after all the times his name has come up in the last two days. I may even—"

Melanie, startled to hear her cell's music, grabbed it out of her purse. "Cindy, what?" Melanie got up, signaled to Mitch to eat his lunch, and then stepped outside so she could hear. Ten minutes later she returned with a frown on her face. Slumping into her chair, she clutched the edge of the table, and closed her eyes.

"Melanie, what's the matter?" Mitch put his hand over hers.

"That was Cindy. I told you about her, my real estate buddy. She's house sitting for me and took over my clients. Seems one of the couples, the Bradys, is balking at the closing date. May cancel completely. Mr. Brady was trouble from day one. Cindy says I have to come back to get the sale on track."

"She can't handle it?"

"That's just it. Brady says he'll only deal with me. That I promised him certain things and they haven't been done. My dilemma is that it was a big sale—$545,000. My commission is the majority of the money I used to fund my trip to Alaska. We were so sure it would go through that my boss paid me the commission, and now, if the sale doesn't happen I have to return the money immediately."

"Not good. When do you have to go?"

"Tonight. It's going to take a few weeks to get the sale on track, if at all, and set a new closing. I have to get the contractors to honor their commitments, and make sure the jobs are completed as promised. The paperwork is ready to go. So as soon as Brady accepts the work, it's only a matter of getting the lawyers and the bank to agree on a date, and, of course, Brady." Melanie sighed and shook her head. "I'll take a cab back to the lodge, grab my stuff, and drive my rental car to the airport. Cindy already booked me a flight—she knows how much this trip means to me. She said the sooner I see Brady the sooner I can get back up here."

~ ~ ~

FRANKLIN HUNG up the phone.

"What's the matter, Dad. Bad news?" Derek helped himself to another scoop of scalloped potatoes.

"Yes. That was doc. It seems Miss Beckett may miss the party. She has to fly back to Florida for a few weeks—a business matter of some sort. I was looking forward to meeting her, but I'm not going to change the date. Doc thought she might return in time."

Chapter 24

Daytona Beach, Florida

A BLAST OF warm humid air enveloped Melanie as she walked from the plane onto the jetway. *Ah, Florida,* she thought, taking off her coat and then her sweater. She saw Cindy standing near the baggage claim, and waved. Stepping off the escalator, the two friends grasped each other in a fierce hug.

"Honestly, Melanie, you are a sight for my bleary eyes. Gideon is going to be so happy to know you're back. He's really lost without his top agent."

The two women gossiped away, like birds chirping in the trees. During the hour-and-a-half ride from Orlando to Daytona Beach, Melanie filled Cindy in on the revelation that her father was a miner in Alaska and had apparently changed his name. When Cindy stopped the car in the driveway, Melanie climbed out and stared at her house. *Please tell me what you know,* she thought, looking from window to window.

"Come on, kiddo, let's go in," Cindy said. "I may not be the best housekeeper, but I did try extra hard yesterday. You must be bushed flying all night. I set up a meeting at ten o'clock this morning with you and Mr. and Mrs. Brady. If you want to take a nap, I can push it to one."

"No, don't do that. I want to meet with them as soon as possible to see where things stand, then I can take a nap. But I do want to see Mr. Gideon later this afternoon so he knows I'm on it. The sooner I can get this closing completed the sooner I can fly back to Alaska."

~ ~ ~

THE SITUATION with Mr. Brady was worse than she thought. Only half of the issues raised by the home inspection had been resolved and the other half left something to be desired. Melanie asked Mr. Brady to give her a day to get some answers, and then to meet with her the next morning at the same time, ten o'clock.

She spent the next five hours on the telephone troubleshooting and making appointments for the following morning at the house to get things turned around.

"Cindy, call Mr. Brady and tell him I'm meeting several contractors tomorrow morning so I have to postpone our meeting until two o'clock."

"He's not going to want to hear from me, Mel."

"I realize that, but I want you to give him the news that we are both working on his issues so you can regain his trust. Also, call the lawyers and the bank and set a tentative date for the closing in four weeks on that Friday … wait. No, make it Thursday. I want to get back to Anchorage on Friday. There's something I have to attend on Saturday if at all possible."

"Do you think all the work will be done by then?" Cindy asked. She was skeptical that Melanie could whip the workers into shape that fast.

"There's nothing major, like taking out a wall. Some paint, a replacement of a couple of fans, a new AC unit … if I keep on it they are all doable," Melanie said, tapping her pencil on the yellow pad of paper, phone to her ear. She returned the receiver to the cradle—no answer.

Cindy went to her office to set up another closing date, and Melanie called Mitch.

"Hey, thanks for calling. You must be bushed," he said.

"Same words from Cindy. I'm tired but right now the adrenaline is pumping. There's an outside chance I can get everything done in time to make it back to Anchorage for the party. I've asked Cindy to reschedule the closing for the Thursday before the party."

"Melanie, don't kill yourself. It's not like there won't be other parties. On the other hand, I miss our midnight rendezvous for hot milk." Mitch chuckled but his words sounded very sweet to Melanie.

"I miss you too, Mitch. Thanks for being so understanding. But, I really want to meet Barrington and I can't think of a better time or place—a party at his house."

"I hear you. Be sure to let me know what flight you'll be coming in on. I'll pick you up. And, missy, that doesn't mean I don't want to hear from you before then … let me know how things are going … and—"

"I'll be back before you can empty two gallons of milk." *Oh, my,* she thought. *I really miss him.*

~ ~ ~

THE NEXT THREE weeks flew by. Melanie and Cindy met Mr. and Mrs. Brady again at the house to show them the progress of the various outstanding issues. Mr. Brady wasn't convinced it could all be accomplished by the following Thursday, but he didn't ask to have the closing date changed.

On Sunday, Melanie took Cindy out to dinner at the Ocean Deck. The temperature hovered around sixty-seven so they ate their mahi-mahi inside and schemed how they were going to get the house ready by Wednesday for a second inspection and closing the next day.

Knowing they had a big day scheduled for Monday, they left the restaurant and Melanie drove them home by way of A1A skirting the ocean. She loved driving this road with glimpses of the ocean between the coral, pale-yellow, and sky-blue multi-story condos and hotels along the shore. Tonight her thoughts were on a different body of water—Cook Inlet, Alaska.

The two women entered the house and threw their keys on the hall table.

"How about a nightcap, my friend?" Cindy asked.

"You go ahead, but I'm going to warm up a cup of milk."

"What's with you and warm milk all of sudden?" Cindy asked. She didn't wait for an answer as she poured herself a small glass of red wine. "I'm taking my idea of warm milk to bed. See you in the morning."

"Cindy," Melanie called. "Did you pick up the mail yesterday?"

"No, I forgot. We were wrapped up with the Brady's. I'll grab it in the morning."

"I'll get it. Mitch said he was sending me something—concerning the party I told you about."

"Okay. Night."

Melanie put on her white sweater and smiled thinking of her parka with the white fur around her face. She ambled down the front steps and across the lawn. The mailbox was silhouetted on the other side of the street like the rest of the houses. It was a beautiful, starry night. Not a cloud in the sky.

Melanie started across the street when out of nowhere a car came careening around the corner heading straight at her. She tried to get out of the way, diving back to the curb lined with grass. She felt a stabbing pain in her arm as she rolled over. Panting, her heart racing, she lifted her head to see the car speeding away but the taillights disappeared around the curve in the road.

Trembling, she managed to get to her knees and then to stand. She tried to brush the dirt and debris from her sweater and jeans but her left arm hurt when she tried to lift it. She shook her head trying to erase an image that popped in her mind. "No, no. Go away." Tears sprang from her eyes as she stumbled into the house, slammed the door shut behind her and leaned back against it. The sobbing wouldn't stop as she slid down the wooden door to the floor.

Cindy heard her cries and rushed from her bedroom. Melanie was sitting on the floor, one hand in her lap, the other lying limp beside her, her head back against the door.

"Melanie, hey, what happened?" Cindy knelt by her friend, put her arm around her but pulled back when Melanie cried out in pain.

"Mel, what happened?"

"My mother. My mother."

"What about your mother?"

"A car just hit me. He didn't see me. I was almost killed. Like my mother."

Chapter 25

Anchorage, Alaska

MELANIE WALKED briskly off the plane and down to the baggage claim area. She saw Mitch waiting for her, a big smile on his face, his arms outstretched welcoming her. She ran to him and he enfolded her with a strong grip taking care not to press against her left side, her bruised arm still on the mend.

"I missed you, Miss Beckett," he whispered in her ear. Leaning back he looked into her eyes. His smile faded as he saw an odd expression on her face. She put her forehead down on his chest, her hands clinging to the front of his parka. "Hey, what's the matter?" he asked, his arms circling her shoulders.

"Get me out of here, Mitch. I'll tell you after we're on the highway," she said, her voice muffled next to his parka.

Relieving her right arm of her tote, he grasped her hand and led her to the baggage carousel. He snatched her bag as it swung by, and then they walked quickly to the parking garage. Mitch kept looking at her out of the corner of his eyes. Neither said a word. Within thirty minutes of her deplaning Mitch turned onto the highway out of Anchorage to Palmer.

Melanie leaned her head back on the headrest, her breathing slowed. She closed her eyes as Mitch covered her left hand with his fingers dwarfing her hand under his. Opening her eyes at his touch, she turned her head a little on the headrest to see his face.

"I missed you, Mitch. A lot. How can that be? We've only known each other a little over two months, yet I feel—"

"You feel like you've known me all your life? Because that's how I feel. Let's not question how long we've known each other, or whether it's possible that we're growing fonder of each other every day. For now, let's accept our feelings for what they are—a feeling that I want you with me every minute, and when you're not, I want time to hurry along so we'll be together again."

Melanie smiled at him and whispered, "Sounds like a plan, doctor."

"Why don't you close your eyes. We'll talk when we get to the lodge. I, for one, am ready for a hot mug of milk."

Melanie smiled and shut her eyes.

The black SUV sped down the highway, through the tunnel of snow banks in the minus five-degree temperature. While she was in Florida, another foot of snow was added to that already on the ground. Mitch reached around to the backseat and pulled Melanie's parka up front draping it over her. She pulled the fur to her face snuggling under the parka's down-filled fabric. A tear escaped her left eye and slowly meandered down her cheek.

In less than an hour, Mitch pulled into the Eagles Nest parking lot and eased into a parking space near the front entrance. It was just ten o'clock and Cathy and Tom had left the outdoor floodlights on. The lodge looked like a movie set nestled under the snow. Feeling the motion of the car come to a stop, Melanie opened her eyes and waited for Mitch to come around to her side and help her out. Cathy stood at the front door, carefully gave Melanie a hug, and told them to run along—Tom would bring Melanie's bags to her room. She said with a twinkle in her eye, that there was a fresh half-gallon of milk and warm apple pie in the kitchen waiting for them. She locked the front door and returned to her bedroom.

~ ~ ~

FIFTEEN MINUTES LATER Melanie padded into the kitchen. Mitch had their milk on the stove, and two nice wedges of apple pie on the table with a fork lying next to the plates. Melanie walked up to Mitch as he was pouring the milk into the mugs, laid her head on his back and put her arms around him in a tight hug.

He turned, lifted her chin and kissed her lips. "I've been waiting for our kitchen escape. Now you sit down and I'll bring our milk over, plus I spotted a brick of sharp cheddar in the fridge. Sound good to you?"

Melanie nodded, yes, and slid onto her chair, laying her hand on the table by his plate—offering him to hold it. Mitch brought over a few slices of cheese, sat down, and picked up her hand kissing her fingers. Raising his mug to hers he then took a sip and set the mug back down on the table. Leaning forward, he turned his chair and looked Melanie in the eye.

"Tell me how you bruised your arm. All you would say on the phone was that it was an accident and you'd fill me in later."

"I was hit by a car. I felt the whoosh of the car as it passed me, lying on the ground when I dove to the side of the road. It was only then I felt the pain."

"Did you get the license plate ... a description of the car?"

"No. It was after 9:30. At night. Cindy and I had had a very long day and we didn't feel like cooking so we went out to dinner. When we got back to the house we were both so tired that she took a glass of wine to bed and I fixed, now don't laugh, a glass of warm milk." She smiled and leaned forward into his kiss. "This was Sunday night and—"

"Sweetheart, why didn't you call me? Sunday. Geez."

"Mitch, I was so scared. Cindy was great and stayed with me until I stopped shaking ... stopped crying. Silly, really. She took me to the emergency room. They took x-rays which showed it was just a nasty bruise. The doctor said it was not broken, but he gave me a sling to wear for a few days. It's only purple and yellow now and doesn't hurt." She took a sip of milk and looked back at Mitch.

"But what was really scary is that I had a flash of my mother, crying in pain. She was hit by a car, on that same road, late at night ... killed."

Melanie looked at Mitch, searching his face for answers he couldn't give.

"Oh, baby, I'm so sorry."

"At first I thought it was an accident. The driver didn't see me. But, Mitch, I've gone over those few seconds time and time again. That car was aiming for me. Someone tried to kill me."

Melanie's words hung in the air. Mitch put the pie back in the refrigerator and their empty mugs in the sink.

"Come on young lady. You're staying in my room tonight. I want you to sleep. We'll talk more in the morning."

Mitch laid next to Melanie all night, his eyes never closing as he listened to her even breathing. Something was very wrong, and he felt it had to do with the search for her father. She had touched a nerve. But whose, and why would they want to stop her so badly that they were willing to kill her?

Chapter 26

MELANIE SLOWLY opened her eyes. For a second she didn't know where she was, and then she remembered how Mitch had tucked her into his bed, cradling her in his arms. She reached for his pillow and pressed it to her body. As she did so she heard the crinkle of paper. Raising up on her elbow, she saw he had left her a note: "I'll wait for you in the dining room. No hurry. We'll take a ride and figure our next move."

"Our next move." "Our" … what a lovely word, she thought. Suddenly energized, she popped out of bed. Dressing quickly, she bounced down the stairs to the dining room. Standing in the doorway a moment, she smiled at the sight of Mitch and Cathy in an animated conversation.

Cathy nodded in her direction and Mitch turned, seeing her, his smile beamed back to her.

"Good morning. Coffee?" Cathy asked.

"Yes, please." Melanie sat down in the chair next to where Mitch had set a plate of blueberry pancakes. They were the only guests in the lodge. It was just ten days until Christmas, and tonight she and Mitch were going to a party.

"I told Cathy we may be staying in Anchorage for a few days," Mitch said taking his seat. "We'll get back to her in a few hours after we've made our plans."

"We rarely have guests from now until after Christmas," Cathy said. "Let me know when you'll be here so I can plan the menus." She scooted back through the swinging door into the kitchen.

"Good morning, sleepy head. Any bad dreams?"

"Not a one. Seems Sir Lancelot slew the dragons."

Mitch gave her a quick peck on the cheek as she helped herself to pancakes from the stack on the platter, adding melted butter and warm maple syrup over the top.

"Sun's almost up—it's going to be a bright sunny day," Mitch said. "I asked Cathy if we could rent the snowmobile for a couple of hours. Tom is checking the gas now—unless you'd rather we take the car."

"Oh, no. This Florida girl isn't passing up an invitation to go snowmobiling."

"Put on a couple of sweaters under your parka, and of course those sexy boots with the heavy socks you bought. Did you see my note?"

"Sure did, Doctor. Sounds like a prescription for some fun," she said smiling.

~ ~ ~

MELANIE SAT behind Mitch, her arms wrapped around his big frame. He drove in a zigzag pattern up the gentle slope of the mountain, the snowmobile's powerful motor roared kicking up a rooster tail behind them on the turns. Coming to a level section he pulled to a stop and helped Melanie off. Reaching in a compartment behind her, he pulled out a blanket and a piece of heavy green tarp.

"We can sit for awhile. If you get chilly, we'll leave but I think the sun will help. Did I see Cathy give you a thermos of coffee?"

"Yes, you did but there's only the lid for a cup. I guess we'll have to share," she said with a twinkle in her eye.

Mitch grabbed her to him, lowered his lips to hers. The embrace was sweet but turned to fire. He pulled away, holding her tight. "Sorry ... I've been thinking of kissing you since I left you sleeping ... a beautiful golden-haired angel."

Melanie sighed. "I'm glad you acted on that thought." She leaned in and planted a quick kiss on his lips. "Now, Doctor, I think we'd better share that coffee and move to another subject. The thermos is in my backpack—can you reach it?" she asked turning around.

Mitch fished out the small thermos and handed it to Melanie. He folded the blanket so there was just enough for the two of them but plenty of fabric to keep the chill of the snow away with the tarp as a barrier. Settling on the blanket, they looked down the slope of the mountain to the lodge below, the snow sparkling in the sunshine. Melanie thought she had found heaven. Taking a sip of coffee, she handed the cup to Mitch.

"Tell me if I'm wrong, but your life was pretty tame until you started searching for your father," Mitch said, looking off at the sky.

"Oh, Mitch ... since the day I stood in front of that house, looking at the picture of my parents and then back up at the house to be sure it was one and the same, my life changed forever. That day I came alive and since then—" Melanie stopped talking and looked up at Mitch. He looked down, gently pushed the fur from her parka to the side of her face and bent down kissing her warm eager lips.

"You were saying ..." he said, his eyes warm from their embrace.

"I was saying," she said in a husky voice, her eyes returning his warmth, "that when I flew to Alaska, I met this wonderful man who took me under his wing ... and ... things really began to happen."

"Things?" he asked, picking up her gloved hand and tucking it under his armpit for warmth. "Maybe we'd better talk strategically or we'll never get off this mountain," he said putting her hand back in her lap.

"You're right, Dr. O'Reilly. Well, there's the rumor—I still haven't forgiven you for not telling me the story when you first knew my last name was Beckett," she said looking at him, pretending to be peeved which ended with a quick kiss on his cheek.

"I'm sorry about that, but I think I know how to make amends."

"Stick to the subject, doc. But the person who really changed my father's mysterious disappearance was Gus— telling me he had changed his name to Andy Bennett. Monday, I'm going to call the people I've met with so far to ask them to check for this different name. Also, it's time I call the Usibelli Mine in Healy. That is one of the few mines that's been in operation since my father disappeared until the time he would have retired."

"That's a good idea," he said filling their cup again and handing it to her.

Melanie accepted the cup from Mitch, took a sip and then cradled it in her mittens. "When Gus said he changed his name, you have to ask, why. Gus seemed to think he was afraid of something. And, don't forget my Aunt Helen didn't like my father—thought he was trouble and that something was wrong. She thought my mother was afraid, acted afraid. And Alice said the same thing, but nobody knows what they were afraid of. So, everybody we've talked to has used that word— *afraid*. I think that fear in this case, raises the stakes—maybe a crime, a cover up."

"The only living link, that we know of, to your father is Franklin Barrington, which also means Derek. I don't know why, but I've never warmed up to Derek."

"I noticed you stiffen when he first came up to us in the cafe in Cordova—when you introduced us. I can't say I had any vibes from him one way or the other. But Franklin Barrington? Why would he care ... after all these years?"

"I don't know, hon, but—"

Melanie looked up at Mitch, then leaned over and kissed his cheek.

"What?" he said.

"Oh, nothing ... *hon*." She laughed when he raised his eyebrows.

"Now listen, you. Stop looking at me with those big blue eyes or we'll table this conversation and go back to when we climbed off the snowmobile," he said grinning. He reached for the thermos and poured the last of the coffee into the empty cup.

"I'm glad Barrington invited us to the party tonight. I want to meet him and talk some more to Derek. Actually, I'm more than glad. I want to see if I can get some information from him. I bought a killer dress for the party ... black ... long ... silky."

Mitch groaned, rolling his eyes. "I had another thought, but black, long, and silky took me off track."

"Come on, Dr. O'Reilly," she teased, punching his shoulder.

"Ah yes. Well, you've been very open that you're here to find your father. So, that's out there—common knowledge. Have you said anything about buying your parent's house and finding the box with the quilt, the leather pouch with the rock, or the lock of hair?"

"Only to you and Cindy. That's not right. Aunt Helen, Alice Peterburse—people in Daytona Beach. But no one up here other than you. No, wait—Gus."

"Okay. As for Gus, do you think he's told anybody else about your father changing his name?"

"I have no way of knowing, but given the way he divulged the secret, I don't think so. He acted like he gave his word to my father that he would never to tell anyone that he was really Arthur Beckett. He even whispered this to me. And again, I've only told you and Cindy." Melanie took another sip of coffee. "Mitch. Just so you know, I do trust you," she said glancing over at him, squinting from the sun in her eyes.

"I appreciate your saying that because I have another thought. It will probably be late when we leave the party tonight. How about we go back to my condo in Anchorage … and then you stay with me. I'm worried about your safety."

"Um, let's see. Safety. What about you? Will I be safe from you?"

"Very funny. And for you to know, I have a spare bedroom."

"Well, in that case, I accept your offer."

"Good." He turned to face her, picking up both of her hands covered with mittens. "Melanie, your safety is nothing to joke about. You said that the car was aiming for you—your words."

"There's something else I haven't mentioned."

"What?" he asked his brows furrowing.

"I may have a case of paranoia, but lately, I've felt I was being followed."

"Like when. Where?"

"The first time was the day after we were in Cordova. I left the Anchorage Daily News to meet you. I was walking down the street and had a feeling ... I turned around several times but didn't see any—"

"What else?" Mitch asked.

"After I returned to Florida, there were a couple of calls where no one was on the other end. I asked Cindy if she had any calls like that. She said no. Then, of course, the car—" Melanie touched her arm where she was bruised.

"Well, from here on keep your radar up. I'd like to ask you to keep in touch with me so I can watch your back so to speak. Is that okay with you?" Mitch asked.

"Not only is it okay but I was going to ask you if you minded if I kept you aware of what I was doing, who I was meeting with, and where I was going. When you hugged me as I stepped off the plane yesterday ... I finally felt safe. Thank you for being there for me."

He lifted her mitten hands to his chest, leaned over, and kissed her forehead.

"Now, Miss Beckett, my bottom is getting cold so you must be freezing. Let's drive this snow buster back to the lodge and take advantage of Cathy's hot tub."

Chapter 27

Palmer, Alaska

MELANIE HUMMED, *Deck the Halls*, as she dressed for the Barrington party—new dress, new shoes, and best of all a handsome doctor escorting her to the gala of the season. Looking in the mirror, she pulled the strands of her blonde hair curling over her left ear to one side and pushed the crystal-studded comb into place. Twisting her head to see if she liked the effect, she heard a soft rap on her door.

Opening the door, Cathy, with a beautiful mink cape draped over her arms and a smile to match, extended her arms to Melanie.

"I couldn't let you walk into the Barrington mansion without the proper wrap. Would you like to wear this?" Cathy said, as she twirled Melanie around and laid the mink over her shoulders.

"Oh, my God, Cathy, it's beautiful," Melanie said caressing the fur.

"You're beautiful. And, that dress—"

"With this cape." Melanie giggled hugging Cathy.

~ ~ ~

PULLING OUT of the Eagles Nest parking lot Mitch switched the car's headlights to high beam and turned onto the highway leading to Anchorage. The night air was a crisp eight degrees, skies clear, and the traffic light moving at seventy miles per hour. Because of the occasional ice patches where the plow didn't scrape to the road's surface, he played it safe not exceeding the speed limit. He reached for Melanie's hand bringing it to his lips.

"*You* are going to set off the gossip mongers tonight."

"Um, you think? Maybe because of my escort— Anchorage's most handsome eligible bachelor, a Dr. Mitchell

O'Reilly." Melanie, raised his hand covering hers kissing it softly.

"And, that perfume—"

"Chanel, darling, Chanel," Melanie said mimicking the late Gloria Swanson.

Mitch looked over at Melanie and was suddenly blinded by the headlights of an approaching semi. He gently tapped the brakes noting his speed had exceeded seventy-five.

"Melanie, brace yourself!" he shouted. "No brakes. No brakes." The road bending to the right was covered with an icy patch. The car began to swerve as Mitch tried to navigate the turn. The truck driver blasted his horn and then laid on it as his front bumper smashed into the back end of Mitch's car as it spun around throwing it up on the bank of snow.

"Melanie, are you hurt?" Mitch yelled, desperation in his voice as he unhooked his seatbelt.

"I'm … I'm okay." Her heart racing and breathing rapidly. Turning to look at Mitch she saw a trickle of blood on his forehead. "Mitch, you're bleeding."

Putting his hand up, he felt the blood. Reaching into his pocket he pulled out his handkerchief and blotted his forehead. "It doesn't hurt. Probably cut it on the steering wheel. You sure you're all right—"

"Hey, buddy, you guys okay in there?" The driver of the semi yelled, pounding on Mitch's window.

"Yeah. You?"

"Yeah. Let's get you and the misses out of the car."

With the help of the driver, Mitch shoved his door open and got out of the car. He helped Melanie over the console and carried her to the street.

"I called the Staties," the driver said. "Should be here any minute. You guys sure you're okay? Scared me to death when you started swerving. God help me, I had nowhere to go."

"My brakes were gone," Mitch said.

Headlights from a squad car, preceded by its siren, pulled up in back of the truck followed by a fire engine and a wrecker.

Chapter 28

MITCH TOOK a deep breath as he entered the city limits of Anchorage. "I owe Cathy and Tom a big one. They must have broken all speed limits—here we are, driving one of their cars and only thirty minutes late. You're sure you still want to go to this party? We could skip it and go to my condo."

"No way," Melanie said. "Besides, after a couple of drinks to settle the nerves, we'll be as good as new. That bandage on your forehead gives you a certain air of sophistication—the bachelor protecting his lady. Now guess who'll be the hot topic of the gossip mongers."

Mitch turned into the Barrington driveway and was greeted with an enormous pine tree sparkling with hundreds of colored lights. The shoveled drive wound around the tree ending to one side of a three-car garage.

"Will you look at that tree," Mitch said slowing the car.

"The only time I've seen one that big was at Rockefeller Center in New York City. This one is even more spectacular with the snow on the branches." Melanie leaned against Mitch to get a better look and gave him a peck on the cheek.

The parking area reserved for guests was full so Mitch swung around and pulled off to the side where a plow had widened the drive to accommodate additional cars. He parked in front of another SUV leaving room for others to pass but allowing him to coast if necessary on the slight grade.

"Looks like all of Anchorage were invited," Melanie said wrapping the mink cape tighter around her shoulders. Cathy had insisted she borrow the fur, chiding she'd never been to the Barrington mansion but at least her cape would hang out with the Anchorage elite.

Taking the keys out of the ignition, Mitch turned to Melanie. "Before we go in I just want to tell you once more how beautiful you look tonight. I'll be lucky if I get one dance with you."

"Thank you, Lancelot. Tom's shirt fits nicely—not a drop of blood to be seen. And I must say you cut a dashing figure in your tux."

"When Franklin Barrington throws a party he really throws a party, and it's usually very formal."

"I'm looking forward to meeting everyone in their finery."

"Remember our game plan—you're not sure what you're going to do. You've had no success in finding your father. And—"

"And—"

"And, I'm sure some busybody is going to wonder about us."

"Oh, but, Lancelot, Guinevere would never kiss and tell." After giving him one last peck on the cheek, she pulled a hanky from her purse. "Here, you'd better wipe off the evidence or I'll surely be caught in a lie," she said bathing him in her smile.

~ ~ ~

FRANKLIN LOVED to throw lavish parties—the sparkle of his crystal chandeliers, the sparkle of the ladies diamonds matched only by the gaiety of the conversation. The Barrington mansion was ablaze with tiny white lights twisted around garlands entwined between the spindles of the curved staircase, Christmas trees in every room and on plants brought in for the occasion. Groupings of red, pink, white, and variegated poinsettia were at the base of each tree as well as tucked around the staging for the musicians. Music from the big-band era drifted out of the solarium.

Mitch helped Melanie off with her fur and handed the cape to the attendant, receiving a numbered ticket in return. Melanie caught her image on the wall of mirrors to one side of the foyer. She saw a woman with blonde hair pulled back on one side. Her black velvet dress clung loosely to her curves leaving one shoulder bare, and flowing to a satin flounce from the knee to the floor. An opening in the flounce on one side accommodated her graceful movement. The dress cut a deep V in the back almost to her waist. Her only jewelry was a pair of diamond stud earrings Mitch had given her before they left the lodge. A black filmy scarf held by a diamond clip at the top of her left shoulder cascaded loosely over her arm camouflaging the bruise as long as she didn't try a frisky Latin cha-cha.

Putting his hand on her bare back, Mitch stepped closer and whispered in her ear, "I may have to throw you over my shoulder and haul you away with me. And, here comes Franklin Barrington. That's a lecherous smile if I ever saw one."

Melanie answered him with a smile, raised eyebrows, and then turned to the gentleman with silver sideburns approaching her.

"Mitch, you made it and this must be Melanie Beckett. You are lovely, my dear." Franklin raised her hand to his lips placing a quick kiss on her fingers. "Come in. Come in." He threaded her arm through his and started walking toward a large group of people. A waiter carrying a silver tray with champagne flutes appeared in front of them. "Would you like a glass of champagne, Melanie?"

"Yes, thank you. Mr. Barrington—"

"Please, call me Franklin, my dear."

As per their plan, Mitch hung back—waiting, watching as people came up to meet the gorgeous newcomer.

"Your home is beautiful—all the tiny white lights—like thousands of diamonds."

Through an archway, Melanie saw guests dancing on gleaming white marble floors. A dark-haired beauty sang a Cole Porter ballad, *Night and Day*, accompanied by a six-piece band. The air was crisp yet carried a scent of lilies from the numerous bouquets on various sized tables placed here and there in every room she entered.

"Now, Dad, I'll not let you monopolize Miss Beckett. Melanie, would you like to dance?"

"Will I have a chance to talk to you later, Franklin?" Melanie asked.

"Of course, my dear. I want to introduce you to some of my guests. Don't keep her away too long, son."

Melanie put her champagne flute down on a table as Derek led her closer to the dancers. Taking her in his arms, he smiled and asked, "Where have you been keeping yourself? I ran into you at a café with the doc and then saw nothing of you for weeks."

"I had to go back to Florida—a quick trip."

"Business or pleasure?"

"Unfortunately, it was business."

"Oh, where do you work?"

"I'm a real estate agent. One of my sales hit a snag so I had to intervene to make sure the property closed."

"I see. Well, I hope you didn't have too much trouble—closing the deal."

"No, everything went quite smoothly. And, you, Derek? What have you been up to?"

"Ah, well, I guess you know I manage the Barrington Mining Corporation."

"I've read about your operation. It's huge and must keep you hopping."

"Have you had any luck in finding your father?"

"Nothing but dead ends. Nobody's seen or heard from him for years I'm afraid. Mitch said he asked your father to look into your old records. I guess he didn't come across a Beckett or we would have heard."

"That's right. I personally checked—a Beckett never worked for us." Circling the floor with Derek, Melanie noticed that Mitch was talking on his cell phone, a frown on his face.

The music ended and the band left the area for a break. Waiters with their silver trays slowly walked through the couples offering more champagne. A bar was set up in the dining room for those who wanted other types of alcoholic drinks. Derek lifted two flutes, handing one to Melanie just as a woman walked up to them.

"Derek, you've been holding out on me. I thought I knew all your friends."

"Sid, nice to see you. I'd like you to meet Melanie Beckett. Melanie this is Sydney Jackman, an old friend of mine."

"Melanie, you can't be from around here with that tan." Sydney chuckled as she helped herself to a glass of champagne.

"You're right. I'm from Florida."

"What in God's name are you doing in this icebox?"

"I'm trying to find my father."

"Any luck?"

"None."

"What a lovely scarf." Sydney picked up the fabric revealing the large bruise on Melanie's arm. "Oh, my, sorry. That is nasty. Must hurt like the dickens."

"It did in the beginning."

"Well, let me know if I can help with your search. I'm a reporter, and at night," she looked around at the guests. "I run down leads for my stories or other people's stories. You can reach me at the ADN."

"Excuse me, ADN?"

"Anchorage Daily News."

"Of course."

The band reassembled and the singer caressed the microphone with her rendition of a favorite Peggy Lee ballad, *Fever*.

"Melanie, may I cut into this little group and ask you to share a dance with an old man?"

Melanie set her glass on the table by her elbow, and smiling back at Derek and Sid, slipped into a slow dance with Franklin.

"I hear you're trying to find your father. You know Artie and I worked for a time together as very young men."

"I did hear a rumor. But, I've talked to so many people, I can't remember who it was. Actually, I believe I heard the story from more than one. Of course, Barrington Mining Corporation and, you, Franklin, are legendary."

"So, you haven't been able to locate your father, or come up with any ideas where he might be?"

"No. Nothing so far."

"You sound disheartened, Melanie. Are you giving up?"

"Oh, no, Franklin." Melanie looked up sharply at the older gentleman. *I'll never give up,* she thought. *I wonder if you're holding out on me, Mr. Barrington. What do you know?* "I asked Derek if you had any record of his working for you over the years. He said—"

"What makes you think he was a miner ... in Alaska, my dear?"

"Oh, a family friend ... she knew my parents ... somewhat."

"And your mother?"

Melanie averted her eyes. She hadn't expected his question—the vision of her mother's lock of hair suddenly washed over her. She felt her eyes tearing. Blinking several times she regained control and turned back to Franklin.

"My dear, I didn't mean to upset you," he said.

"You didn't." Melanie looked down. "I ... my mother is dead. Killed. I was two months old." Melanie breathed deeply several times and looked back up at Franklin.

His eyes were wide, mouth open slightly but said nothing. A waiter stepped in front of them and Franklin, shaking his head once, offered her a glass of champagne which she accepted. He picked up another glass and took a long swallow, emptying half of the slender flute.

"I'm sorry to hear that ... about your mother."

~ ~ ~

SYDNEY, A CHAMPAGNE FLUTE in one hand and eyebrow cocked, tapped Derek on the shoulder. He turned to her as she licked the rim of her glass and then offered him a sip.

"Aren't you going to ask me to dance?" She lowered the flute from his lips to hers and again licked the rim.

Without answering, he removed the glass from her hand and set it on the tray of a passing waiter. Taking her in his arms they began to dance.

"You're a temptress, Sid," he smiled down at her, holding her so tight to his body he felt every curve and suddenly wanted more. Thinking better of it, he eased his grip on her back.

"I've missed you, Derek. You didn't call for weeks, and then out of the blue you have a little assignment for me."

"I've been busy." He twirled her around and back into his grasp.

"Um. I've been thinking … about my assignment. And, I asked myself, 'why is Derek so interested in the Beckett woman?'"

"And did you come up with an answer?" Derek again threw her body into a twirl and back to him, bending her back and up into his arms once again.

"I did. I know what you want, Derek. I can help."

"How do you know what I want."

"Oh, I know. And once I help you get it—"

He again twirled her out, but this time he pulled her back against him, desire rising.

Sid breathed softly in his ear, feeling his passion. "We're alike you and I. We'd be good together."

Chapter 29

FRANKLIN WAVED goodbye to his last guest as they drove down the driveway leaving the multitude of twinkling lights in their car's rearview mirrors. Closing the front door, he ambled down to his study and poured himself a nightcap. Settling into his favorite easy chair in front of the fireplace, he stared at the crackling flames. Franklin preferred a wood fire over the gas installed in Derek's den. Swirling the amber liquid around in the brandy snifter, he ruminated over the evening.

He felt the party had added to the gaiety of the season especially after he checked the number of bottles of champagne his guests had consumed. He hoped they all arrived home safely. His thoughts were interrupted when his son entered the room.

Seeing his father with a drink, Derek stepped over to the wet bar and helped himself to a snifter of brandy. He joined his father in front of the fireplace and sat in a matching chair after dragging a footstool in front of him and planting his feet up on it.

"Well, Dad, you did it again. That was a helluva party, maybe surpassing the former Barrington Christmas parties."

"I always enjoy seeing our friends at their glittering best. The Beckett woman is quite beautiful don't you think?" Franklin said, glancing up at his son.

"I suppose so."

Looking back at the flames licking a large log, Franklin murmured, "I hope she finds her father."

"Did I hear you right? You hope Melanie finds Arthur Beckett? You can't be serious." Derek tossed down his drink and strode over to refill the glass. "Tell me, *Dad*, of all the stories going around about you, Tommy Barnes and Artie Beckett, which one is true? Did you help Barnes down the rock slide—that seems to be the most logical to me. Did you?"

Derek stood to the other side of the fireplace, leering at his father. "Well?"

"Ah, Derek, that was a long time ago."

"Yeah, well if you did, and let's say Artie saw you, he could come forward and accuse you of murder."

"Really, Derek. Watch your tongue." Franklin's fingers tightened under the bowl of his glass. *I'm sure he did see me nudge those rocks, but they were loose—still how could I have done such a thing … and how could I have … stop it, Franklin. You're traveling down that rat hole again. Senseless. Doesn't change anything except bring on your depression. Again.*

Derek stalked around the room, stopping only to take another swallow of brandy. "Yeah, that's what happened. Old Artie saw you and ran. Where was he when Tommy fell?" Derek stopped in his tracks and threw a piercing look at his father, a father that looked very small in his overstuffed chair.

"As I said, it was a long time ago, but as I recall … several yards away, up on a ledge. From his angle he could have thought I had something to do with Tommy's fall … I suppose."

"That Melanie woman is nothing but trouble. She finds her old man. Talks him into coming after you. After me. After the company—"

"Derek, stop it. Stop talking like your grandfather—a madman. Always out for himself. Greedy to a fault. Never a hint of compassion."

"Well, if I'm like him I take that as a compliment. Look at the company he built."

"Your memory is a bit warped, my boy. The company took off after I took over. When he crashed his plane into that mountain peak I didn't shed a tear."

"Well, I did. He believed in me. Not like you. I've had enough of your tutelage—those years down in the mineshafts, digging the dirty black rocks from yet another blast, tossing them into the rail car. I'm lucky I didn't get trapped. You insisted I work for those other companies to see how they operated. It's time you name me vice president. Yeah, Senior Vice President of Operations. Let's start the new year off right."

"You're not ready, Derek. Your judgment leaves something to be desired. Did you invite Sid tonight? I know she was not on the guest list." *He'll never take over Barrington Mining Corporation. He's headstrong, greedy, cuts corners,* Franklin thought, watching his only child pace around in front of him.

"Yes, I invited her. She does a job for me now and then? Damn good operator ... someone I trust."

"Well, I don't trust her ... not sure why. She always seems to be hiding something when I talk to her which isn't very often. We avoid each other, but tonight. We had to say hello and goodbye. And now, I'll say goodnight to you. I'll ask Henry to lock up and make sure the fires are out. See you in the morning."

~ ~ ~

"SEE YOU in the morning," Derek mimicked. He sat in his father's chair, scrunching his rump around until he was comfortable. A flame caught his eye ... hypnotized he began mumbling to himself. "I can't let Melanie find her father. Of course, he could be dead anyway for all I know. But if she did manage to find him ... I don't care what Dad says, I'm sure he pushed ... let me amend that ... killed Tommy so he could take the gold find home to his daddy. He's turned soft. He used to be hard as the rocks he blasts in those black holes. I either have to stop Melanie, or if she finds her father, then I have to stop old Artie for good before he destroys Barrington, my Barrington."

Derek set his empty glass on the table next to his father's. The room was warm and he was suddenly very tired. "I must call Sid in the morning and ..." Yawning, he looked around the opulent room, smiled, then staggered down the hall to his bedroom.

Chapter 30

Anchorage, Alaska

MITCH HELPED Melanie out of the car in his parking garage and on up to his condo. She snuggled into his protective arms as he fumbled with his keys finally unlocking the door. Even though it was well after midnight, the city of Anchorage lay before them through his wall of windows. The city resplendent with its mantle of holiday lights looked like a jewel against the black velvet night.

"You must be exhausted, hon," Mitch said throwing his keys onto the hall table.

"The adrenalin has definitely faded."

Carrying her overnight case, he led her to his guest bedroom and set the case on the luggage rack.

"How about we rendezvous in your kitchen," Melanie suggested. "Say in ten minutes for our version of a hot toddy. I want to change into my flannel PJs, fluffy pink slippers, and—"

"Sounds like a Cinderella moment. I'll be waiting." He kissed her lips softly and headed for his bedroom. Melanie gave the door a push and entered the walk-in closet to hang up Cathy's fur and to peel off her evening gown. Then she dressed for comfort and warmth and padded in her slippers to the kitchen.

Mitch, now dressed in a black-flannel jogging suit, was pouring the warm milk into their mugs when she leaned against his back and wrapped her arms around him.

"Hey, watch out. I could get to like this arrangement. I may have to lock you up here in my tower."

"Lancelot," she said dreamily, "can we have our milk and cookies in the living room. Your view of the city is breathtaking."

"Sure, come on. Those cookies you mentioned are in that bag by the toaster."

Settled side by side on the couch, they tapped their mugs, each taking a sip as they gazed out the expansive glass to the city lying below.

"Tell me what you thought about the party, and Franklin," Mitch asked, resting his head on the back of the couch. "He seemed quite taken with you."

"It's hard to believe he and his son have the same blood—so different. First of all, the party was spectacular—the setting, the dresses, the jewelry—my God, you'd think there were diamond mines in Alaska instead of coal."

"In these parts, a few people think of coal as black diamonds."

"I liked Franklin. I felt his warmth and thought it was genuine. Whereas Derek, while nice and gentlemanly, seemed conniving. He really peppered me with questions and who is Sid? I know she said she worked for the newspaper, but I got the impression she had other sidelines." Melanie took another sip from her mug.

"I've only met her once before. While some of the people there tonight are patients of mine, she isn't one of them. Did you learn anything about your father?"

"No. But Franklin seemed very melancholy when he spoke of working with him. Knowing the story about the three friends, I can't see him having anything to do with Tommy Barnes's death. He's too soft."

"Hon, don't let tonight fool you. You don't build a corporation like Barrington's without being a tough guy. I guess in his day, he was as brutal as his old man is rumored to have been. I never met the senior Barrington. Our paths never crossed. I had all I could handle with finishing my internship and joining my old man's practice."

"That's the first time you've mentioned your father. He was a doctor, too?"

Mitch leaned forward, elbows on his knees as he looked out at the city. "He was an alkie with a brusque bedside manner."

"Not like you at all," Melanie said softly.

"There was a time, when I first worked with him, that we were very much alike. I was an alcoholic, too." He paused, took in a deep breath and turned to face Melanie. "Went to AA. Went through the twelve steps. I'm afraid it's in my genes."

"I didn't realize ... you've ordered a glass of wine at times when we've had dinner out."

"But you never saw me drink it. I wasn't ready to tell you. Just because I don't is no reason for you not to enjoy having a drink when you feel like it."

"But you quit."

"One day my father and I had an argument over a diagnosis of a very sick woman. We were into the cocktail hour—that day the hour was ten in the morning. He bellowed that the woman suffered from one thing and I yelled back it was another. Of course, the treatments were drastically different. Two weeks later the woman died. I tied one on for over a month. Didn't see any patients, never called my father or my mother. I was picked up for drunk driving and thrown in jail to sober up. It wasn't the first time. Seeing the demons that night ... well, I finally made it home. I was living with my parents at the time. So I packed a suitcase and left Juneau."

"Do your parents still live there?"

"Mom does. Dad had one drink too many and drove head-on into a brick wall. I ended up here in Anchorage and started a new practice. I'm just thankful I got out in time before I totally screwed up my life, or a patient's, or ended like my dad killing himself behind the wheel of a car."

"Your work ... taking care of the miners with black lung, I noticed you never asked for payment."

"My practice has done extremely well which allows me to help the miners pro bono. There's not much I can do for them ... can't cure them, but I can help make their days a little more comfortable. From time to time I'll ask them to come to a clinic, if there's one where they live. Try a little rehabilitation—exercise, nutrition, testing their heart."

Mitch set his mug on the coffee table and turned to Melanie. "I have to talk to you about Cordova ... what happened that night." He took her hand in both of his, staring down.

"I learned from Martha, at the home where you met Tony and Sam, that a long-time patient, a friend, Scott Baker had died a few days earlier. He was only sixty-nine. He'd worked in the mines all his life, down in the shaft. He had black lung bad—I tried to help, to keep him out of the hospital which he couldn't pay for."

Mitch looked up at Melanie. She knew he was reliving the last day he saw his friend alive. "I'm not trying to excuse my drinking that night at the Rose Lodge—there's never a reason bad enough for me to take a drink ... but this time ... I wasn't prepared. Scott was always urging me to open a rehab center—like I told you about when we flew to Cordova. He and I had long discussions about how I could help the miners with black lung."

Mitch looked away, out the window, then down to her hand, and finally up to her eyes. "Melanie, he left me everything he had saved over those years in the mines—$48,000. Martha gave me a note, hand-written by Scott telling me where to find his will. The note ... he wanted me to start the rehab center we had talked about with his savings."

Melanie leaned forward, touched his cheek and raised his hand to her lips as she looked back into his pained face.

"The thought of losing him ... I tried to reign in my emotions but they spiraled out of control. After I said goodnight to you, I went down to the bar. I thought one drink would help ease the turmoil I was feeling—but for an alcoholic there is no such thing as one drink. I wasn't honest with you a few minutes ago when I said I was an alcoholic. I am an alcoholic. An alcoholic you cared for when I fell into your arms."

"Mitch, I—"

"In the morning when you were in the shower, I went to a nearby church. I called a friend and he met me there—we've helped each other through some rough spots. He stayed with me for two hours—stayed with me until I gathered the courage to face you. Yet ... I didn't have the courage to ... Melanie, I'm so sorry. Can you forgive me?"

"Mitch, I cared that night for a friend in distress. Forgive you? Forgive you for what? I felt blessed that it was me you came to that night for comfort. There's nothing for me to forgive—you have to forgive yourself."

"Melanie, you're the most wonderful thing that has ever happened to me. I knew the minute I saw you at the Eagles Nest that morning—knew that my life had changed that instant."

Mitch took her shoulders, bringing her lips to his. Melanie wrapped her arms around his neck responding to his embrace with an intensity she didn't believe possible. He stood, pulling her against his body. "Melanie, my dear sweet Melanie, I love you." Holding her face in his hands he kissed her forehead, eyes, cheek, neck ... Melanie I want you."

He lifted her, her arms clinging to him, pressing her breasts to his chest, and carried her to his bed, laying her on the blue satin quilt. He removed the fluffy pink slippers, the flannel pajamas, and his jogging suit.

He looked down at her as she held her arms up inviting him to make love to her. "You are so beautiful ... my beautiful, beautiful angel." He kissed her deeply, caressed her body, matched her moans of love with his own until not able to hold back another moment, they received each other completely and fully, knowing they had made a bond that would never be broken.

Chapter 31

THE AROMA of fresh brewed coffee wafted into Mitch's bedroom. He reached for Melanie but the bed was empty. He stepped to his bathroom and grabbed his navy-blue bathrobe tying the belt around his waist. He followed the scent of coffee now combined with toast to the kitchen.

Melanie stood at the stove humming as she cracked a second egg into the frying pan. Mitch circled his arms around her leaning his cheek against hers. Melanie leaned back into him as she sprinkled salt and pepper on the eggs, lowered the heat on the burner and turned into Mitch's embrace.

"Now who's the sleepyhead," she said. "How do you like your eggs?" she asked her eyes filled with the warmth of a woman in love.

"Just like this—in the kitchen with you in my arms."

"Oops, excuse me. Have to butter the toast. If you'll set the table, I'll serve up our breakfast. We have some planning to do, Doctor."

Mitch put out the knives and forks and poured the coffee. "I'll have to pick up some cream for you—sorry, all I have is this powdered kind."

Melanie set his plate on the table, gave him a quick peck on his lips and rubbed the reddish stubble on his chin.

"Hey, are we going to eat or play?" he asked smiling at her as she pulled away. She sat down at the table and took a sip of coffee, eyeing him over the rim of the mug.

Receiving his answer, he sat down chuckling. "Okay, Beckett, what are you planning?"

"Much as your invitation to stay here would be wonderful, I want to head back to the lodge. I'm going to call the Usibelli Mining in Healy now that we have two names to ask about—Arthur Beckett and Andy Bennett. And you have patients to see. As you say, you have bills to pay. I've been taking up a lot of your time."

"Melanie," he said reaching across the table for her hand. "We were lucky last night."

"I know. I saw you talking on your cell at the party. Was it about the car?"

"Yes. Tom and Cathy went with the wrecker to a service station in Palmer. One of the attendants drove them home. By the way, they said no problem with us borrowing their car until I rent one."

"I don't know what we'd do without those two," Melanie said, putting another piece of bread in the toaster.

"Tom said the whole back end of my car is smashed in. The truck barely had a scratch. I'm sure the insurance guy will see it as not worth repairing. But that's not why Tom called."

"What else?"

"The brake lines were cut."

Melanie's head snapped up. She looked into Mitch's eyes, realizing the impact of what he just said. "Someone tried to kill us?" she whispered.

Mitch sighed. "I don't see any other way of looking at it. I have patients lined up today and tomorrow and then I'll be back at the lodge with you. I close the office for the holidays—last three weeks of December. So after tomorrow we attend to emergencies only."

"We?"

"Yes. There are three of us. We each have our own practice but cover for one another. It so happened, when you came along—" Mitch set his fork down, picked up her hand across the table and pressed it to his cheek. "When you came along, one of the guys had just returned from a trip to Hawaii. I covered for him while he was away and he was on call for me when we flew to Cordova and the other side trips—Houston and Sutton. So, my calendar is open through New Year's Day. You have Cathy's car. If you take me to a rental place this morning—"

"I miss you already ... you'll be back at the lodge by tomorrow night?" she asked.

"Yes, and promise me you'll let me know where you are at all times. If I'm with a patient, send a text message. But,

Melanie, if you feel threatened, let me know immediately. In fact, after last night, I'm going to call a police officer who moonlights as a detective. He'll check my car, see if anything else is amiss besides the brake lines. If he agrees with Tom, that the lines were cut, I'll file a police report. But, his main mission will be to keep an eye on you, from a distance, until I can get to the lodge. You'll never know he's there unless he senses you need his assistance. Is that okay with you?"

Melanie looked out the window but saw her reflection. The sun wouldn't rise for another two hours. "Normally, I wouldn't want that. But, I guess we're not talking normal." She looked away from the window and back at Mitch as she touched the bruise on her arm. "I guess that sounds like the prudent thing to do. That would give me a little more freedom if I want to run into town, or if I do end up driving to Healy. I won't be afraid to leave the lodge. But tell him to go on his way when he sees you arrive."

"Good. By the way, I'm picking up Niki. The trainer said she's catching on fast—working with the other dogs, pulling as a team. He thinks she has the instincts and the smarts to be a lead husky soon. Which brings me to Christmas. You haven't said whether you're planning to stay here or return to Florida."

Melanie swept around the table and planted herself in his lap. Taking his whiskered chin in her fingers, she carefully kissed his lips. With a twinkle in her eyes and a broad smile on her face, she said, "One of those mama grizzlies I've heard about, couldn't drag me away. What do you have in mind?"

She hopped off his lap and refilled their coffee cups.

"A real Alaskan holiday. And I'd like to get out of town so we can relax without looking over our shoulder every minute. Do you think you'd like to mush with a dogsled team?"

She set her cup down, eyes wide with surprise. "I'd love it. Will Niki be part of the team? How many dogs? Do I ride on the sled? Where do we go?"

"Whoa," he laughed. "Yes, Niki will be on the team. It'll give me a chance to see her in action. And, yes, you'll ride in the basket this trip. Remember when we flew to Cordova—"

"I loved Woodstock."

"I mentioned the bushman, Clarence, and that I had spent the last four Christmases with him?"

"Oh, Mitch, are we going to see Clarence—a real bushman. We have to go—he must be expecting you?"

"Well, I'm sure he is. I told him in September that I'd mush over on Christmas day and spend the night."

"Then it's settled. Do I have to go shopping again?"

"We both do. I have most of the mandatory equipment— headlamp, snowshoes—we'll have to pick up a second pair for you. We have eight days—only six by the time I join you at the lodge with Niki. I usually follow the Junior Iditarod trail—teens race from Wasilla to Yentna Station, seventy-five miles, and back. So there's a trail of sorts that we'll follow. The trail passes over the Susitna River and Clarence lives a couple of miles up the river where he built a log cabin. When we get to the river we'll turn off the junior trail."

"It sounds like fun."

"It will be, but things can happen in the wilderness. It's not the same as sledding down a hill in your backyard, well, certainly not in your backyard. But we can make it in a day easily. From four to six hours if we don't break down, or run into a moose."

"A moose?"

"Yup. You'll have to help me watch the trail—a fallen tree, a possible hole in the ice, and, of course, a moose. They wander down the trail to the river. They will stand their ground. Not good if the dogs tangle with one. A few sled dogs are killed every winter by an angry moose. I'll have my gun— almost everyone who goes into the wilderness to hunt and fish, or just hiking, carries a gun for protection from the animals. We try to avoid them, or skirt around if we can, or shoot in the air to scare them off. Trouble is they don't scare easily."

Chapter 32

MELANIE WAS now a permanent guest at the Eagles Nest. Cathy gave her a key, a run of the kitchen, and the use of her choice of vehicles—SUV, snowmobile, or dogsled. In return Melanie advised them on the purchase and sale of properties in and around Anchorage, Palmer and Sutton.

Melanie's conviction gained strength every day as she tackled the search for her father. Returning from her night with Mitch and the heady social whirl of Anchorage, thanks to Franklin Barrington's party, she had a new sense of purpose. She and Mitch talked on their cell phones several times a day. He had more appointments than he thought and wasn't going to be able to get away until the weekend—four days instead of two before they would be together.

Melanie called the Usibelli Mine Company in Healy. She spoke with a clerk in the personnel office who said she couldn't divulge employee information. Melanie pleaded explaining the situation and that the man she was looking for would probably have retired over ten years ago. To make less of an issue for the clerk, Melanie added that the man was probably dead. After that the clerk said she'd check with her boss, and she thought, given that the man was elderly and maybe dead, perhaps she would be given permission to help.

The woman called back four hours later. There was no record of Arthur Beckett, but she did find an Andy Bennett who worked at the mine for twenty-five years until he retired eleven years ago. His last known address was a post office box in Wasilla.

Melanie was stunned and at the same time ecstatic. She thanked the clerk and immediately turned on her laptop and checked the internet again. But Andy Bennett did not appear in any directory. Borrowing Cathy's SUV, Melanie took a run up to

Wasilla. The post office would not divulge any information regarding the rental of a post office box. The attendant would not confirm or deny that an Andy Bennett had rented a box. Arthur Beckett, AKA Andy Bennett, had vanished. None the less, Melanie felt for the first time since Gus had talked with her at the Sutton Library that she was getting closer. She called Mitch from the car and talked so fast, her voice filled with excitement, that he laughed and told her he would be waiting for her at the lodge. She had a thirty-minute drive.

Melanie's mind was swirling with possibilities but she had no idea what to do next. Her cell rang pulling her back from the images flitting around in her head.

"Mel, you there? It's Cindy."

"Cindy, hi. You wouldn't believe how beautiful it is here. We had fresh snow last night—it's a fairyland. What's up?"

"Yeah, well you won't believe this either. I was taking stock of the pantry cupboard where you stashed all the canned stuff. I came across a colorful tin box, about the size of a shoe box. It was behind two big cans of ground coffee. Very old cans."

"And … what was in the tin?"

"Letters. Love letters from one Arthur Beckett to one Lorna Mae Thompson."

"Oh My God, Cindy. Did you read them?"

"Yes—I didn't think you'd mind. Mel, they are beautiful. Do you have time—can I read you one?"

"Yes, yes, please. I'm on my way back to the lodge … go ahead."

"Okay, this is dated July 7, 1966. 'My dear Lorna Mae, it does not seem possible that even as you read this note I am speeding northward away from you. You who are dearer to me than anything else on earth. Each mile that is added to the many which will eventually lie between us also adds string upon string to my heart drawing it back to you. But the day is coming when I will return, and Lorna Mae dear, it's in my heart that it will be to you. I love you dear, love you more than I can tell, a steadfast and unchanging love, and surely dear girl, God does not put such love into a man's heart without sooner or later having that love answered in kind'—"

"Cindy, stop." Melanie, tears rolling down her face and dropping to her red sweater, pulled a tissue from the console. She tried to mop the tears, but they kept coming. "Cindy, can I ask you a big favor?"

"Anything."

"Can you make copies and overnight them to me at the address I left you for the lodge?"

~ ~ ~

MELANIE PULLED into the Eagles Nest driveway and into the open garage. She jumped out of the car and raced to the door leading to the kitchen. Mitch was sitting at the table having coffee with Cathy when she burst through the door. Mitch immediately stood up and Melanie flew into his arms, kissed him on the cheek, and took a step back.

"I have so much to tell you."

"Wow, that was a nice entrance," Cathy said. "Before you guys disappear, you had two telephone calls, Melanie."

"Who called? Any message?"

"First was a man. Said he had some information for you, were you here, etcetera. I told him you had gone to Wasilla and would be back later. He hung up. No chance to ask him if he'd like to leave a message. The second was a woman, younger than the man, asked the same thing and she also hung up. Here are the numbers. I jotted them down from the telephone's incoming call list, but the Caller ID displayed Unknown. Sorry that's all I have."

"Thanks, Cathy. I'll try the numbers—see if I can find out who called."

"Cathy, why don't you sleep in tomorrow morning," Mitch said. "Melanie and I have some serious shopping to do in Wasilla with only three days to Christmas. I'd like to leave for Wasilla by seven in the morning. We can pick up breakfast there."

"Thanks, I just may do that. Don't worry about Niki. Tom's already in love with your dog. Now he's threatening to get me a team for Christmas." She laughed as she went to the stove to stir the chili.

"That would be some present. Mitch, let's go upstairs so I can change," Melanie said, grabbing his hand and pulling him to the door. "I feel like an Eskimo with all these layers."

~ ~ ~

A BLACK SEDAN had pulled out of the post office parking lot soon after Melanie left and followed about a quarter-mile behind her. After she entered the lodge, the sedan made a U-turn in the Eagles Nest parking lot, pulled out onto the highway, and headed west toward Anchorage.

Chapter 33

Wasilla, Alaska

MITCH QUIETLY slid from Melanie's bed and tiptoed down to the kitchen. He set the coffee to brewing, put two whole-wheat bagels in the toaster, and loaded a tray with a small creamer, raspberry jam, napkins and a knife. Waiting for the coffee to finish brewing, he scanned his shopping list. They had a big day ahead preparing for the dogsled run to the bushman on Christmas morning.

Pouring the coffee into a small thermos he went upstairs with the tray pushing Melanie's door open with his toe.

Hearing Mitch's footsteps on the creaky stairs, Melanie sat up in bed and stretched.

"Whoa, Lancelot. Do you need some help there?"

"Everything is under control, but don't bounce around." Carefully sliding onto the bed, he set the tray down between them and then leaned into her eager lips for a quick kiss. "Good morning, love."

"When will we see the sun this morning?" she asked, slathering a spoonful of jam on her bagel.

"Around 10:30. We'll have five hours of sun today so we should reach a toasty eight degrees."

"Toasty, huh." She smiled, taking a sip of coffee and another bite of bagel. "Are we taking Niki with us?"

"Not on your life. She'd pester the daylights out of us scampering around in circles. I swear she knows when we're getting ready for a run. You haven't seen my car. It's full of gear I keep stored at the condo, so I'll be ready, or partially so, for my next mush. Here's the list of what I have and the checklist for what we need." Mitch pulled out a piece of paper from his bathrobe pocket and reached for another list lying on the bedside table.

"I've made a partial list for you—like some new wool socks for Clarence. He'll fall short of some supplies before the breakup."

"Breakup?" Melanie added a dab of jam to her bagel.

"That's when the ice pack on the lakes and rivers really starts to *break* apart. By spring, if the ice is gone, Clarence can take his little boat down the river to get what he needs. Being it's Christmas I'd like to take him some new clothes. I've put those on your list. I'm 6-foot-two, 212 pounds. He's five-foot-eleven and slim. It's a hard life he's chosen, but he says he loves it. I don't think he weighs more than 165. He can always use more socks. Hang on a minute. He gave me a list in September. Let me run to my room." Mitch gave Melanie a quick kiss on the cheek and jogged down the hall.

Melanie popped out of bed, grabbed her briefcase, and slipped quickly back under the covers pulling her knees to her chest and then the quilt up to her shoulders. Retrieving a pen and pad of paper from her case, she jotted down what Mitch had told her about Clarence's size, plus a few other notes.

"He thinks he's going to run short of powdered milk—that's on my list," Mitch said sliding under the covers next to Melanie. "The main items we have to get will be for the dogs. Todd, he's Niki's trainer, is carting over the team. We shop today, put everything together tomorrow, and leave the next morning, Christmas. That's when we rendezvous with Todd. He'll help me put the harnesses, and ganglines, booties—"

"Booties?"

"A musher's prime concern is his dogs—their paws are particularly prone to injury," Mitch said. "They can get cut on the ice, snowballs form between their toes, as well as plain old abrasions from the ice crystals. The booties come in several different fabrics depending primarily on the distance you expect to travel. We aren't going very far—around forty miles—so we don't need booties for a long distance. On a trip like ours, some mushers won't use them but you never know when a dog might get hurt. The booties are like a pocket—two pieces of cloth sewn together."

They finished their bagels and Melanie drank the last drop of her coffee.

"Time to get dressed and hit the road," Mitch said, stealing a quick kiss. "I'll meet you out at the car. Thirty minutes okay?"

"You bet, Mr. Musher. But I want to pet Niki before we leave."

~ ~ ~

AN HOUR LATER, Mitch parked the car in front of the Mushers Feed and Supply Store in Wasilla. "The owners of this store are very helpful so if you can't find something, or you want to check on sizes for Clarence, just ask," Mitch said sliding out of the car. "Do you have your list?"

"You bet I do. I'm sure they'll spot me as novice right away," she said, as they walked hand-in-hand up the walkway to the entrance.

"After this adventure, you'll know more about mushing than most in these parts."

Entering the store, a bootie sign was off to his right. Mitch walked to the bin and pulled out a black bootie made of Polar fleece bunting and showed it to Melanie. "Here's what we were talking about earlier. This Velcro strip winds around the dog's leg. But, you have to be careful—too tight and you cut off the circulation. Too loose and they fly off the dog's foot. Putting on the booties is where you can help Todd and me."

"Great. I want to help as much as I can. I may be clumsy at first, but I want to try. Mitch, this is going to be so much fun." Melanie looked around, then stood on tiptoe and kissed his cheek.

"Let's just hope the weather holds. So far the projections are good," he said.

"Hey, Mitch, I was wondering when you'd be in for supplies." A woman hustled up to Mitch, hand extended. "And who might this be?"

"Sarah, I'd like you to meet Melanie Beckett—a musher in training." He put his arm around Melanie's shoulders in a bear hug.

"Well, hello, Melanie. Are you going with Mitch to visit the bushman?"

"Yes, I am. He gave me a list I have to fill so I'll probably be peppering you with questions." Melanie chuckled along with Sarah.

"That's our doc … lists, lists, lists. You just flag me down when you need help." Mitch handed Sarah a list of dog supplies. Looking at the list she headed toward the back of the store with Mitch on her heels. "We just got a shipment of Yukon chums, forty cents a pound. The dogs will love them. You can take the salmon whole or chop them on the trail. Trouble is the team will want to stop more often for their treats I dare say. Do you want us to sharpen your ax before you go?"

"Yes. It's in the car. Melanie is going along for the ride this time, so I'm borrowing a sled from the Eagles Nest. It's the toboggan type, sits on the runners. There will still be plenty of room for our supplies, if not I'll trail a small toboggan behind."

"Have some nice Delta straw for your team—how long are you staying with the bushman?"

"Only one night. Clarence said last September that he'd cut some pine branches for the dogs, so I'll skip the straw."

"RedPaw Dog Food just came in. The mushers are swearing by it. Hope to do a good business when it's time for them to stock up for the Iditarod this March. They swear it helps the pads of the dogs' feet and different formulas are available for endurance depending on what the musher thinks a dog needs. And, oh, I have the ground lamb and fish you like so much to cook up with their dog food. Oh, oh. Here comes Melanie and look at that load of clothes she has in that basket would you."

"I found everything but Mitch you have to take a look at some of the sizes. Tell me what you think."

"Think? I think my bushman is going to have one helluva Christmas."

"Hang on, there's my cell." Melanie fumbled in her parka's pocket, the star war's music playing softly. "Hello. Who is this! Stop it. Stop!" She slammed the top of the phone shut. Her breathing was fast as she quickly looked around the store.

"Hey, everything okay?" Sarah said. "Anything I can help with?"

"No. It was a prank call. The person wasn't very nice." Melanie looked at Mitch. "I'll tell you later, but right now, let's see what you think about these clothes." Melanie picked up a pair of lined wool trousers and handed them to Mitch, a forced smile on her face.

Mitch looked at her, concerned, but determined she didn't want to talk until they left the store. He turned back to Sarah. "I need a new cooker for the dog food and Melanie needs a slip-on parka without a zipper."

"No zipper?" Melanie's eyes widened.

"Yeah, zippers ice up and you can't get out of the parka if you have to change on the trail."

~ ~ ~

A GRAY SUV pulled into the far side of the parking lot. The driver scrunched down, sipping a hot cup of coffee.

Chapter 34

Anchorage – Barrington Mansion

SQUATTING ON THE FLOOR, Franklin continued to rummage around in the back of his long walk-in closet. "So many boxes," he muttered. "Why do I keep all this stuff? Oh, so this is where I put those goggles and my scarf. I think Derek gave it to me … maybe … no, no, it was Ashley."

Franklin rocked back on his heels, and then sat down on the plush gray carpet crossing his ankles. He caressed the red angora muffler. "Ah, Ashley. You tried so hard to be a good wife. But, I was always off doing … doing what? You were left alone so much."

Franklin lifted the box to his lap and carefully pawed through the contents. Near the bottom, he picked up a sweater, knitted from the same yarn as the muffler, folded over several times. He felt something inside the folds. Carefully laying back the arms of the sweater and then the bottom edge, he uncovered a picture of his late wife—a dark-haired beauty of twenty-six at the time the photograph was taken.

He traced her face with his fingers—lightly touching the glass that protected her. She was smiling at him, a loving look in her eyes. There was an inscription in the lower right-hand corner. He squinted but couldn't make out the writing. Reaching into the breast pocket of his green flannel shirt, he pulled out his glasses. Perching them on the end of his nose, he again looked at the inscription: "Merry Christmas my dear, with all my love, Ashley."

Franklin's eyes misted. Leaning back against the trousers hanging from the rod above, he cradled the picture to his chest.

"Ashley, Ashley, Ashley—how stupid I was, always looking for love in another woman's arms. Searching. And there you were—what I was searching for was beside me all the while. How foolish of me. My dearest, forgive me."

Franklin, stiff from squatting and then sitting on the floor, struggled to his feet. Carrying the picture he ambled into the bedroom. Wiping the glass with the soft cloth of his shirt, he placed the picture on his mahogany dresser. He gazed at it for a moment, then turned back to the closet.

Boxes were stacking up behind him as he opened and closed one after the other. "Where is that costume?" he muttered. Frustrated, he tossed yet another box behind him. In front of him was a clear-plastic bin and he could see that it contained colorful objects—mainly brilliant orange.

"Here it is." Franklin gleefully picked up the box and carefully made his way around the debris he had piled up and set it on his black-velour bedspread. "Now, Cyrano, you are going to come back to life. That was some Halloween ball, my friend. Better than any Mardi Gras I've been to. Yes, Franklin, my boy, you certainly know how to throw a party," he said chuckling.

He threw a black wig on the bed along with the mustache, but left the nose and the cape in the bin. He was really only after the mustache, but maybe the wig would come in handy. Darting back into the closet, he pulled back the hangers holding his various parkas. He needed one especially big so he would look fat. The rest of his winter gear was in the closet by the garage. Later he would ask Cook to see that his bedroom closet was put back in order.

Picking up the mustache, he walked into his dressing room and peered into the mirror. He pushed the adhesive side to his upper lip, then stepped back. "Yes," he mumbled. "That should do it. Wasilla. That's where the person at the lodge said Melanie and Mitch had gone this morning. They needed supplies from the Mushers Food store. I'll be able to pick up their trail."

The one thing Franklin knew for sure was that if Artie was still alive, he had to find him before his son did. He had to make things right with Artie. Because he disappeared that day long ago, he was never to realize his share of the gold vein they had found. At the time Franklin didn't care, in fact, Artie disappearing made it easier for Franklin Barrington Mines to stake the claim. But now, seeing things through the eyes of a much wiser old man, Franklin had to make sure the debt was paid. Of course, he could never fully pay the debt—but at least it would be something.

Franklin stared at his image in the mirror, ruminating over his son's actions. Derek was a hothead, greedy to the core like his grandfather. Franklin feared his son was planning something to eliminate any threat to what he felt he was entitled to. Derek had invited Sid to the Christmas party, yet Franklin noticed they hardly spoke a word to each other. He saw the exchange between Derek, Mitch and Melanie. When Sid touched the scarf Melanie wore, revealing a large bruise on Melanie's arm, Sid's face had the cunning look of a witch.

"Yes, I must find Artie before Derek does. Melanie will lead me to him—the love of a daughter searching for a father she never knew."

Franklin walked back into the bedroom and over to the picture of his wife and gazed into her eyes. "Ashley, my dear sweet Ashley … help me. You're out of my reach, but maybe there's still time to right the wrong, as much as I can, of what I did to Artie."

~ ~ ~

IT WAS A LITTLE after noon when a fat man, black hair and mustache, entered the Mushers Supply store. He looked around, a little befuddled.

"Hello, sir. Can I help you find something?" the woman asked.

"Ah, yes. I see you certainly have a complete line of goods for mushers. Was that Dr. O'Reilly I just saw leaving?"

"Yes it was. Do you know him?"

"Oh, my yes, we go way back. Never saw him with a lady before," the man said chuckling.

"He's taking her mushing on Christmas to meet a bushman. Should be fun for her. Won't be a long trip though—he's sticking to the Junior Iditarod trail, being it's her first time and all."

"Oh, yes. That's pretty unless they go up to the Yentna Station—then it gets rather rough," the old man said in a gravelly voice.

"Oh, they're only going to the Susitna River."

"I see. Well, I won't keep you. I wanted to see what you carried for mushers. My son is getting into the sport. Nice chatting with you. Goodbye."

Chapter 35

IT WAS ONE in the morning when Melanie slipped out of bed, wrapped Cathy's heavy bathrobe tight around her, and stepped into her fluffy slippers. She tiptoed down the stairs to the kitchen.

Mitch sat at the kitchen table writing furiously on a yellow pad of paper. He looked up when Melanie pushed through the swinging door. "Couldn't sleep?" he asked smiling. "Sit down—I'll warm up your milk. Cathy is going to begin to wonder about us invading her kitchen almost every night."

"She seems to take everything in stride. What are you writing?"

"After you told me yesterday—that Andy Bennett did in fact exist and worked at the Usibelli mine for so many years, I guess you could say that I caught your excitement. Here's what I'm proposing we do. First, we visit Clarence. The weather forecast is predicting snow flurries tonight which will make everything beautiful for you and your first dogsled excursion Christmas morning." Mitch leaned over giving her a quick peck on the cheek. "I'm so glad you're coming with me."

"Of course, I'm coming with you. Traipsing off into the white wilderness, no 7-Eleven or Holiday Inn in sight—just me, a pack of dogs, and Sir Lancelot." She smiled over the rim of her mug.

"Good. I called Dick, the detective I hired to watch over you. He tailed you to the post office. He didn't see anything suspicious. I gave him the two names, Beckett and Bennett and asked him to do some digging, also to see what he can come up with regarding the post office box. Hopefully, he can pull some strings and find out who picks up the mail. By the way, you never told me about that phone call that upset you yesterday."

Melanie looked down at the table. "I overreacted. Some woman said I should go back to Florida and to stop making a play for Derek. As you heard, I hung up on her."

"Is the number still on your phone?"

"I think so."

"Do you have those phone numbers Cathy gave you yesterday?"

"They're in my room."

"When you get a chance later this morning give them to me and the one on your cell. I'll pass them along to Dick."

"You think they mean something?"

"Let's just say I find it strange someone asked where you were but didn't leave a message."

"Do you think Dick Tracy can find out anything about the post office box?" Melanie asked with a grin.

"Miss Marples, his name isn't Dick Tracy. It happens that Dick Jennings is with the Anchorage Police Department, so I'm hoping he'll have something for us by the time we get back from our little adventure in the wild."

Mitch looked at Melanie just as her eyelids closed. Her head jerked up, eyes opening to narrow slits. She caught him looking at her and yawned.

"I think that milk is kicking in," she said. "What time do you want to start putting our supplies together—all that frozen fish for the team. How many dogs is Todd bringing over?"

"Nine and Niki makes ten. Come on. Let's go back to bed. We'll have a leisurely breakfast about 7:30 and then get to work."

"Wait. You said first we visit your friend Clarence. But you never said what was second."

"Second, when we get back from our Christmas visit, we go to Healy and search in earnest for your dad."

Chapter 36

COOK SETUP the breakfast buffet as Franklin and Derek chatted about their plans for Christmas. What Franklin didn't mention was that he had a busy day ahead of him preparing to follow Melanie and Mitch with a snowmobile. He had a nice one in the garage but hadn't run it for a couple of years, so he had made arrangements to rent a machine in Wasilla.

Helping himself to bacon and eggs, Franklin took his seat at the head of the table.

"Derek, will you bring over the coffee carafe? What are you up to today and tomorrow?"

"I have some errands to do today, and I'm taking a date to the midnight service," Derek said, pouring a refill into his father's coffee cup.

"Church? That's a first," Franklin said, sprinkling salt and pepper on his eggs.

"Well, she strongly suggested we go and then we're going back to her place. You were up early this morning. Something going on?"

"Yes. I've been invited to a midnight service by my friends in Sutton. They're having a party and then off to church. It will be late so I'm going to stay over. Probably stay there most of Christmas day. I know last year you were away through New Year's Day."

"In that case, let's tell Cook to take the day off," Derek said, mopping up his egg yolk with a piece of whole-wheat toast.

Franklin rang the bell sitting on the table in front of him under an evergreen floral arrangement—small red and silver ornaments mixed with pinecones.

Cook bustled in carrying a compote of fresh melon slices. "What can I do for you, Mr. Barrington?" she asked setting the fruit mixture on the table between the two men.

"Cook, it seems my son and I will be gone most of the next couple of days, or at the very least in and out. Why don't you take the next three days for a holiday of your own? In fact, if you'd put together some meals in the refrigerator, you can leave when you finish up this morning. Leave us a list of items so we'll know what to look for. How does that sound to you?"

"Thank you, sir. I'd like that. There's some nice venison sausage and I'll cook-off that caribou roast for you. So you two won't be wanting anything for lunch today?"

"I'll be leaving mid-afternoon sometime," Franklin said. "Have a few things to do before I visit my friends. How about you, Derek? Will you be here for lunch?"

"No. I'm spending the day with the woman I told you about earlier."

"There you have it, Cook, and here's a little something for you." Franklin reached into the inside pocket of his suede smoking-jacket and pulled out a white envelope. "Merry Christmas, Cook."

"Merry Christmas to you, too, sir, and you, Derek."

Chapter 37

IT WAS 8:30 in the morning and still dark. The sun would rise at 10:15. The snow was littered with the items Mitch had taken out of storage—the dog food, and the clothing items for Clarence as well as the powdered milk he asked Mitch to pick up for him on his last visit. Cathy had turned on the parking lot floodlights so they could see what they were doing. Niki romped around, occasionally howling to the wind her nose raised in the air.

Mitch and Melanie looked at the husky. "She knows we're getting ready to go for a run. She won't sleep much tonight," Mitch said. He put on his headlamp and picked up the one he purchased for Melanie. "Here, let me show you how to put this on." Melanie adjusted the strap to fit her head with Mitch's help.

"The floods are good, but you can target the light with the headlamp in the shadows or behind the car. When we get ready to leave Wasilla tomorrow it will be dark. We'll need the lamps for the trail unless we have a full moon."

"What will I be looking out for?" Melanie asked, using the lamp's beam to see what remained in the back of the car.

"Mainly moose or downed trees. Let's put the dog food on that tarp. Can you handle that bag of salmon chums?"

"Yup."

"Drop the tailgate on the car for a platform. Open the chum and put about half of it in this plastic bag," Mitch said handing a large bag to Melanie. "That should be enough for ten hours of treats. The rest will go in Cathy's freezer. When you get it open toss one to Niki. Watch how she nestles in the snow with the salmon between her paws. She bites off a piece at a time—savoring the juicy flavor I guess."

Melanie opened the bag, called Niki, and threw her a piece of the frozen fish. The husky did exactly what Mitch said she would, then licked the tasty residue from her front paws. Melanie divvied up the dog food, the energy bars for herself and Mitch, and then tackled the clothing. Mitch had insisted that she buy another parka—one that was a pullover in case of a storm—no outside snaps or zipper to let the cold air in or that would freeze shut if ice crystals formed on the zipper track. She put her new heavy socks, boot liners, and another pair of mukluks to the side to take into the lodge. The boot liners would go inside her boots for additional protection from the freezing cold.

She saw Mitch drag out the sled from one of the lodge's garage bays and ran to help him. When he got to the car, they lifted it onto the roof and fastened it tight to the rails.

"It's not very heavy," Melanie said, throwing the end of the rope across to Mitch.

"A musher's rule of thumb is that a dog should not pull more than its own weight. Niki is still young but she's almost full grown and weighs forty-five pounds. Because you'll be riding in the sled, with all that extra weight from the Barrington Christmas party—"

"Extra weight? Me? How about you, Doctor? I saw you munching on all those little beef sandwich circles." Melanie picked up a handful of snow and threw it at him.

"Listen here. I'll have you know that those little delicacies were made with caribou meat and—" Mitch ducked as another snowball flew his way.

"You were saying about the weight of the load?"

"Okay, truce. We won't be out on the trail more than five hours each day which is a walk in the park for Todd's dogs. And, the first part of the trail that we'll be on doesn't go up any mountains. Just a few hills. We can always jump off and help out by pushing which the Iditarod racers have to do quite often when they get in the mountain ranges. That's why I settled on ten dogs including Niki. Are you sweating yet?" Mitch asked.

"I sure am. How did you guess?"

"We've been working for more than three hours, and we have a lot of clothes on. One of the big issues a musher faces on the trail—sweat will freeze next to the skin. Sometimes my clothes are soaked with sweat and I have to change on the trail. Again, we may sweat up a storm, but we'll be at the cabin before the temperature drops so we can change into dry clothes there. Along with your headlamp, be sure you have your goggles handy. That sun will burn your eyes unless you protect them."

Melanie looked around—nothing was left on the snow. "Are we done?" she asked.

"Yeah. I left enough dog food and ground lamb to give Niki a good meal tonight and tomorrow morning. Dehydration is a problem for working dogs. They need lots of water but sometimes won't drink on the trail. So I've been taught to use plenty of water when preparing her food when we're out with a team. I heat up the water, melting the snow, in the cooker and drop in the frozen lamb and a scoop of dog food. She loves it."

Niki, hearing her name scampered over to Mitch, jumped up on him throwing him to the ground. Man and dog rolled on the snow, tussling with each other. Niki barking. Mitch laughing.

Melanie sat down on the snow and chuckled at their faces covered with the white stuff.

~ ~ ~

AT THE END of the day with all their gear packed in the car, Mitch and Melanie took Niki outside to bed her down. He stamped down the snow making an indentation and then filled it with an armload of straw. Melanie watched as Niki circled round and round on the straw, pawed a little, circled some more, then lay down curling into a ball, tail up over her nose.

Mitch knelt down next to his dog and gave her a quick pet. "Sleep well, pretty girl. Tomorrow you're going to have some fun." He stood up, looked down at the curled up husky and turned to Melanie. Grabbing her hand, he said, "How about a quick dip in the hot tub, a glass of warm milk, and then to bed. It's a big day for us, too."

An hour later they were in bed, Melanie curled up in Mitch's arms listening to his rhythmic breathing.

"Mitch, you asleep?"

"Almost. You?" he replied.

"Not quite." She closed her eyes, but they popped open again.

"Mitch?"

"Yeah?

"I'm excited about tomorrow?"

"Me, too."

"Mitch?"

"Yeah?"

"I have something to tell you."

"Okay."

"You know when we were talking ... after Barrington's party?"

"Yeah?"

"Promise me you'll never hold back telling me something for fear I won't understand. I love you, Mitch O'Reilly. I love everything you are, everything you stand for and your dreams of building a rehab center for the miners. I can see it one day as a tribute to your friend who died—the O'Reilly and Baker Respiratory and Rehabilitation Center."

"Melanie?"

"Yes."

"Will you stay and build it with me?"

Mitch turned over to face Melanie, their heads on the pillows inches apart. He gathered her in his arms as the passion rose within them. Christmas Eve melted into the early hours of Christmas morning. The lovers lay sleeping, bodies intertwined and spent.

Chapter 38

IT WAS SEVEN in the morning and dark when Mitch pulled into the parking lot on the far side of the Wasilla general store. A little Christmas tree, colored lights blinking, sat in the bay window. He, Melanie, and Niki hustled into the brightly lit store to wait for Todd with the dog team. A couple of old timers sat around the potbelly stove laughing, kidding each other as they sipped steaming coffee from large mugs.

"I could sure use some of that coffee. How about you, hon?" Mitch asked. He took a quick look around and then saw Todd drive up. "Mel, make that three coffees. Todd's here."

"I'm on my way," she answered.

Mitch and Niki left the store joined quickly by Melanie with the three coffees. She was greeted by barking dogs still in their compartments mounted in a huge container custom fit to the bed of Todd's pickup truck. Noses and front paws protruded through the bars of each compartment's gate. Niki stood beside the truck howling, nose in the air, waiting for her friends to be unloaded. Mitch and Todd were staking pickets where each dog would be anchored. Each dog would then be placed in a harness. The harness would clip to one side or the other of the tugline.

Melanie high fived with Todd—glove to glove—when Mitch introduced her to his friend and trainer.

"Melanie, why don't you go back inside and drink your coffee while Todd and I finish unloading."

"All right, but just for a few minutes. I want to help."

Mitch smiled at her as she trudged through the snow and back into the store to join the gents sitting by the stove.

"Looks to me like Melanie's more than a visitor," Todd said smirking.

"You've got that right. Now wipe the grin off your face and let's get the sled set up," Mitch said, socking his friend's shoulder.

In the store, Melanie pulled up a chair by the heat of the stove and sat down.

"Now, I'd say the day is looking brighter. How are you, little lady?" one of the men asked, chewing on his pipe.

"Cold," Melanie replied smiling.

"Ten below—it's almost a heat wave," the other man said through a mustache over his upper lip, joining his full beard down to the middle of his chest. Both men rested their feet enveloped in heavy boots near the base of the stove.

"You're not from around here, I take it," the first man said pulling his knit cap off his head revealing a braid down his back.

"Florida," Melanie chuckled. "By any chance do either of you know an Andy Bennett?"

"I don't. Do you, Louie," the bearded man asked his friend.

"Nope. Never have. He live around here?"

"I'm not sure. He's a relative I'm trying to track down. I see my friend is packing the sled. Nice chatting with you. Merry Christmas," Melanie said, returning the chair to the corner.

"And Merry Christmas to you, little lady. You come back any time. We'll be here," Louie said pulling his cap on again.

Melanie set the coffee mug in the sink by the coffee maker. Overhead were shelves lined with coffee mugs. *All the regulars must have their own mug,* she thought. *It would be fun someday to line up Mitch's and mine with the others. Maybe another time.*

Joining the guys, she saw the sled was packed, pickets were stuck in the snow, two-by-two, and then the sled at the back of the line. Mitch and Todd, their headlamps on, unloaded the first dog. Todd slipped on his harness and snapped him to a picket in front of the sled. The dog stood barking but did not pull on the picket—obviously trained to wait for his teammates, but he could still bark. Niki joined in the barking but she was still free to run around. Mitch snapped the second dog to a picket alongside the first.

Todd snapped the third and fourth. Mitch slipped the harness on Niki and put her in fifth. Melanie followed the progress as Todd snapped Tiger and Bugsy, the two lead dogs, into place.

"Bugsy is a funny name for a leader," Melanie said, kneeling to watch Todd. "Yeah, well, as a pup he kept chasing the rabbits. He still has a hankering to take off if he sees one, but Tiger's strong and keeps to the trail dragging Bugsy back into line. Tiger's something else. You'll see. Even if the snow has blown over the trail he seems to know it's there. He can smell the other dogs if they've been by like during the Iditarod. But if his team is in the lead he has an uncanny ability to stay on the trail. Each pair of dogs has a duty in the team."

"They don't just play follow the leader?" Melanie asked.

"Oh no. The pair behind the leaders are called swing dogs. They force the rest of the team to swing out, in an arc. If the team followed precisely behind the leaders they would create a sharp turn and get all tangled up in the lines. The rest of the dogs making up the team provide the muscle to pull the sled and for speed. The last two are special again. They're called wheel dogs. They're the first to feel the load as the team starts out. They're usually the biggest but not always. Sometimes a more agile dog has an easier time of keeping out of the way of the sled's runners. All wheel dogs have to be unflappable because of the pounding of the sled's runners close to them. It can be unnerving."

"Do the dogs always run in the same position?"

"No. Mushers will move them around. They're like humans—maybe Bugsy is ornery one day and doesn't want to be next to Tiger. Or, you want to try a dog in the lead position to see if they're smart enough. Take Niki. I think she's going to be strong and smart enough to become a lead dog. Maybe Mitch will give her a try while you're on the trail."

Mitch finished attaching the dogs to the tug line and Todd snapped the back end of the line to the sled—about thirty feet behind Tiger. The dogs were in a frenzy, yelping, barking, and jumping letting Mitch know they were ready to go. Tiger jumped like a Jack-in-the-box--all four legs in the air at once.

"I guess that does it. Thanks, Todd," Mitch said. "I'll give you a call when we're on the trail heading back tomorrow. It will probably be late in the evening—maybe nine. Is that okay with you? We want to spend the better part of the day with Clarence."

"No problem. Have fun. Nice meeting you, Melanie."

"Thanks for telling me how the team works," Melanie called back as Mitch tucked a blanket around her in the sled. The bags holding their supplies lined the bottom of the sled with Melanie secure on top.

Mitch squatted by Melanie's side. "You'll hear me yell the following commands—sometimes they may be laced with a few cuss words," he yelled to her over the dogs howling. "Hike, go, and mush means to get going. Gee—go right. Haw—go left. And whoa, of course, means to stop. There's a brake on the back of the sled next to the runner. It's a claw that digs into the ground." Mitch stood up, looking at the excited team. "I told Max, he's the owner of the general store that we were going to the bushman's cabin. In case we get into the trouble they know where to look." He smiled at her. "You look so pretty with the fur framing your face. Are you warm enough?"

"Very toasty," she shouted. "The hand warmers in my gloves are wonderful." She offered her lips up for another kiss and then Mitch turned to the back of the sled, stood on the runners, and yelled at the top of his lungs at the jumping, yelping, barking dogs.

"HIKE! GO YOU HUSKIES!

The sled quickly picked up speed. Melanie heard the whoosh of the runners on the snow beneath her. The dogs' barking was not as frenzied as they pulled and settled into a trot, then only an occasional yelp was heard. Mitch turned off his headlamp letting the full moon light the way. Tiger and Bugsy had been on this trail several times with Todd and a few with Mitch so they knew the way. Niki trotted along in her middle-of-the-pack position.

~ ~ ~

FRANKLIN FIGURED he was about three hours behind Mitch—at least from what the two guys in the general store said. They also said that the woman was looking for a relative. The owner of the store was more than happy to give him directions and the route that the doc always took to visit the bushman.

Mitch and Melanie are going to be surprised when I show up, Franklin thought as he climbed onto the snowmobile.

Chapter 39

Anchorage, Alaska

DEREK'S DATE with the redhead had been a big success, especially after he gave her a heart-shaped, diamond encrusted pendant on a silver chain—the discount jeweler was running a holiday special. She was staying in Anchorage on a photo shoot for the Discovery Channel. The rest of the crew had returned to their homes in the lower forty-eight. Derek wished he had met her before the Barrington Christmas party. He would have enjoyed showing her off to his father and their guests.

He had taken her to several swanky places for the last couple of weeks and thought she might be ready to acquiesce to his advances. They had skipped the Christmas service at a nearby church, deciding to return to her hotel room for nightcap instead. The nightcap ended with a steamy, wild rolling about in bed. Waking every once in a while resulted in more romping about until they finally fell asleep around four in the morning.

Derek woke with a start, disoriented when his cell phone rang. He had thrown it on the bedside table when he undressed earlier in the night. Grabbing for the phone, he saw it was Sid.

"Sid, this better be important. It's only 8:11, and it's Christmas—" His model friend sleepily wrapped her arms around him.

"What? They took off on a dogsled? Do I care?"

"Come on, Derek," the model whispered kissing his ear. "Hang up."

Derek slid out of bed away from her reach and walked quickly into the bathroom shutting the door.

"They said the woman was looking for a relative?"

"Yes. They're following the Junior Iditarod trail out of Wasilla."

"Okay, I got it. And, Sid, good work. Merry Christmas. You back off. I'll take it from here."

"Is that all I get? 'Good Work. Merry Christmas, Sid.' Come on Derek. How about I fix you dinner, here at my place, when you get finished with this gig? The way I see it, you owe me big. A little time together ... I think you'd like it."

Derek thought about his nights with the redhead. Maybe time to move on. Maybe a few nights with Sid, a willowy brunette. What was it she said at the party, *"We're good together."*

He whispered into the phone, "Yeah, sounds nice. When I get back."

Chapter 40

Wasilla, Alaska—Christmas Morning

IT WAS 10:30, the sun was rising, and Franklin felt like a young buck again. The excitement of driving a snowmobile over the rugged terrain challenging his strength, and the thought he might find his old friend again made him almost giddy. But he was getting way ahead of himself. First, he knew he had to catch up with Melanie and Mitch warning them to watch out for Derek. Maybe after they all returned to Wasilla, Melanie would let him help in the search for her father, include him in their plans.

Franklin had heard doc talk about the bushman and he was looking forward to meeting the old man. He had once thought about living out in the wild, not alone though. He would want a woman, a wife with whom to share the beauty of the country. But his father never gave him the chance, and Ashley would never have considered such an idea.

Franklin supposed he could have waited in Wasilla for Mitch and Melanie to return from the bush, but the thought of making the trip pumped his adrenalin. After all the bushman's cabin wasn't very far away when you consider the vast distances from one place to another in Alaska.

Franklin kept to the trail, following the sled tracks. It was a beautiful morning, snow sparkling in the new sun. The trail turned up through a stand of pines. He marveled at their beauty, limbs heavy with snow.

Chapter 41

"WHOA! WHOA!" Mitch yelled as he stepped on the brake bar. Two metal prongs dug into the snow preventing the sled from running into the two wheel dogs. The team stopped trotting, and took up barking. However, being highly trained they knew it was rest time so they quickly scrunched down into the snow somehow not tangling their lines.

Mitch set the brake hook and trudged through the snow to Melanie, sinking almost to his knees. He was greeted with a smile barely visible through the snow encrusted fur around her face.

Carefully pulling the fur back, he gave her a quick kiss on the lips. "We'll take a twenty minute rest. Here, let me help you up." He took hold of her outstretched hands and pulled her to her feet. "Do you know where we put the salmon chums?" he asked.

"Sure do. I'll dig the bag out."

Melanie pulled the edges of a few bundles aside, and uncovered the one with the frozen fish chunks. Mitch walked down the line praising each dog, giving each a pat or a scratch behind the ears. Returning to the sled, he dug around and found the small bag containing the dog booties.

"Give each dog one salmon chunk and tell him, or her," he smiled, "how great they are. I counted five bare paws. I'll replace the booties while you give them their treat."

"Can I get you something," Melanie asked.

"After we tend to the dogs we'll have a couple of those energy bars and some water. You were leaning against the bag with the water so hopefully you kept them from freezing."

"So that's what I was doing with all this clothing— protecting the water." She laughed and started down the left side of the team of dogs, marveling at how patiently each waited for their turn.

The dogs eagerly accepted the frozen salmon Melanie threw to them. They snatched the treat mid-air and then grasped the chunk between their front paws, savoring each bite. They paid no attention to Mitch as he replaced the lost booties, anchoring the boot with the Velcro around their leg just above their paw.

The dogs tended to, Melanie found the energy bars as Mitch pulled out the water bottles—ice cold but not frozen. Sitting on the sled to rest his legs, Mitch looked back at the terrain they had just passed through and then ahead at the team. Tiger was at least thirty feet away, at the head of the team.

"We're making good time. I figure a little more than ten miles-per-hour." Mitch took a long swallow of water.

"When do you think we'll see the cabin?" Melanie asked, finishing off her bar.

"No more than two hours. Probably less.

"What about water for the dogs?"

"Todd said he mixed a lot of water with their morning meal before we left. I did the same for Niki. The frozen fish will provide some water. Good question, Beckett. Dehydration can be a problem when the dogs are working—like any athlete."

Tiger jumped up and started barking. The rest of the team stood and joined in his chorus.

"I guess they're telling us our rest stop is over," Mitch said chuckling. "Give me your headlamp. We won't need them until tomorrow. Put those wrap-around sunglasses on. We couldn't have asked for a more beautiful day," he said packing away the lamps.

"The snow, the mountains—it's as if we're the only two people on earth, except for the hooping and howling of the team," Melanie said shading her eyes as she looked down the row of dogs.

"Yeah, they're raring to start running." Mitch tucked Melanie back onto the sled, walked around to the runners, released the brake hook and the brake prongs. Stepping on the runners, he yelled to the team to get going.

"Hike. Hike. Go, Tiger. Come on, Niki, you pretty girl. Sarge, you knucklehead, you're a worker." The sled began sliding over the snow picking up speed.

Melanie suddenly raised her arms in the air, pointing off to her right. Mitch looked following the direction of her hand and spotted her reason for alarm. A moose. He was standing off at the edge of the trees about fifty yards away.

"WHOA! WHOA!" Mitch stepped hard on the brake and the sled slowed to a stop. The dogs saw the animal and began barking. Mitch set the brake hook and pulled out his revolver. Circling around to Melanie, he said, "He's far enough away I think we can keep going. I had to be sure he wasn't going to charge because we'd never be able to outrun him. We'll start up again but I'll keep my eye on him. I don't want the dogs to set out chasing him. We may see another one. This trail is known as Moose Alley. Good eyes, Beckett."

Mitch quickly returned to the runners and released the brakes.

"HIKE. HIKE. Tiger, hike."

Tiger started to trot forward but kept looking back at the moose.

"TIGER, HIKE, GO GO."

Tiger turned his head back to the trail and picked up the pace. Reluctantly the other dogs, still barking, pulled as they were trained. Mitch looked back several times, but the moose stood his ground. The terrain was flat and Mitch urged the team on. They flew past the moose. The trail turned at a bend in the river and he was soon out of sight.

Mitch breathed a sigh of relief as the trail turned up a hill, winding through stands of spruce and pine trees. While the surrounding forest was beautiful in the snow the trees made steering tricky. Tiger and Bugsy stuck to the trail, but with Mitch thirty feet behind more than once he planted both feet on one runner to help turn the sled causing a rooster tail of snow to shoot out behind him like a skier in a downhill race.

Melanie knew that Mitch kept his gun in easy reach in case an animal decided to teach them a lesson—this was their domain. No humans allowed.

Chapter 42

DEREK SWUNG into his driveway and screeched to a halt, narrowly missing the garage door as his car slid on the ice. Luck was holding for him.

His mind was whirling—do this, do that, no, not that. Sid deserved a bonus for tracking Mitch and Melanie to the feed store, but most of all finding out they were taking a dogsled trip on Christmas day. One might say, "so what," but not Sid. She was devilishly persistent once she was given an assignment. When she learned they were starting out at the Junior Iditarod trail, she had staked out the general store where the Junior Iditarod trail began, drinking who knows how many cups of coffee, and burning gallons of gas to keep warm. *Yes, she deserves a very big bonus,* he thought chuckling.

Pressing the button on his garage door opener, he darted into the house leaving the car in the driveway. He knew Cook was away and that his father had said he was going to visit friends, so he could race through the house picking up the things he needed without a lot of nosey questions thrown at him.

Running up the stairs to his room, he opened the top dresser drawer and removed his pistol and a couple of clips of ammunition. He then hustled back down the stairs to the closet next to the entrance of the garage where his winter clothes were stored for trekking off on his snowmobile.

Pulling out what he needed, he threw the stuff on the floor behind him, and finally uncovered his heavy boots. *Thank God, I remembered to put the felt liners back in the boots the last time I wore them.*

Satisfied with the extra layer of waterproof pants and parka, and the thermal underwear under everything else, he grabbed the backpack with goggles, sunglasses, and headlamp.

One last dash to the kitchen for some snacks, a thermos with water, and he was set to check out the snowmobile in the garage.

Franklin always hounded him about making sure it was ready for the next outing—gas, always extra gas. Derek would often take it out without his father's knowledge. This was one time he was glad he had followed Franklin's advice—the tank was almost full, and he had topped off the spare.

Derek dashed out to the car, turned it around in the driveway and backed into the bay with the trailer holding the snowmobile—a quick coupling, then pulling the trailer clear of the garage, then pushing the button closing the garage doors. In short order, he was speeding down the road to Wasilla.

In less than an hour, Derek pulled into the parking lot of the general store. He swiftly unloaded the snowmobile, locked his car, and took off over the snow to the start of the Junior Iditarod trail.

Derek loved the speed, the thrill of the turns spraying snow behind him, and the machine's response to his gentle touch. Racing over the sparkling crystals, he was really cruising. His blood pumping—knowing he could catch Melanie at the bushman's cabin. He figured she and Mitch would be arriving there soon, then throwing down a few drinks, never suspecting he was after them. Of course, the dogs would bark. But they were always barking at wolves or other animals that came out at night.

"Wait a minute. What's that?" Derek brought the machine to a stop, jumped off and ran ahead a few yards.

"Looks like snowmobile tracks. But here. A sled," Derek muttered. "Melanie must be driving behind the doc and his dog team. But … why would she do that? Derek, you're so stupid. Doc probably had to haul so much stuff to that crazy bushman there wasn't room for Melanie on the sled. And she wouldn't know how to drive another team of dogs. Shit, they'd drag her all over Alaska."

He chuckled at the thought of Melanie being dragged into the mountains as he took a sip of brandy and then stuffed the flask back in the bag under his seat. A blast of gas to the machine, and he was on his way again.

Derek continued to scheme as the distance closed between him and his prey—less than three hours. He had to figure a way to make Melanie's death an accident. This was perfect really. Doing away with Melanie would stop the endless search for her father—Derek wouldn't care where the old man was, or even if he was alive. The search for Arthur Beckett would end. He would no longer present a threat to Derek or his old man.

"I know what I'll do," he mumbled into the icy wind striking his face protected by a black ski mask. "I'll get a shot off through the window, then make a run for it. They'll think it's some trapper trying to rob them. And, best of all, Melanie will be dead."

Derek adjusted his sunglasses, then gave the machine more gas, speeding faster along the tracks ahead of him.

"At least, that's one idea. Might be better to burst in and shoot them all. Knock over everything. Franklin and I will be toasting the new year before they're ever found."

Chapter 43

"WHOA! WHOA!" Mitch stepped on the brake bar, the team slowed to a trot then stopped and laid down in the snow. Mitch had turned the team out of the trees hoping to put some distance between them and the moose. The dogs were ready for a short rest after racing for almost a half hour along the bank of the frozen river.

Setting the brake hook, he trudged around to Melanie and sat on the edge of the sled next to her legs. They both watched the dogs nestle on the snow.

"You, okay?"

She nodded, yes. "Now that the brown guy with the biggest head of antlers I've ever imagined is out of sight, I can say it was exciting." She leaned forward, as the two parkas came together, somehow their lips found each other through the ice crystals on the fur.

"I think we can make it to Clarence's cabin by one o'clock. We'll spot the smoke from his chimney."

"I can't wait to see how he survives so far from civilization. Is he friendly?"

"Yeah, you'll like him. I'm anxious to see how he's doing. I brought him some new medicine. Last time I saw him, three months ago, his cough was worse. Damn black lung. We'll just stay tonight. I usually stay several days, give him some company. Besides the fishing I've already told you about, we play cards and I help with any repairs he needs. He has a generator for electricity—all the comforts of home—relatively speaking. He doesn't run it much. Conserves the gas."

"I like cards. You play gin or the guy game—stud poker?" Melanie asked.

"Both, and Mexican Train—"

"Ah, dominoes. I know that one. It's so peaceful out here. Oops, was peaceful. Tiger's antsy to get going."

"Melanie, do you see anything back there … on the horizon?"

She scrunched her eyes and looked in the direction Mitch was pointing.

"Like what?"

"I don't know—a moving black dot I guess."

"No. Maybe it's what they call in the desert—a mirage."

"Maybe." Mitch tucked her in, released the brake, the dogs shook their bodies and started trotting.

Melanie was enjoying the ride. *I'm becoming an Alaskan,* she thought smiling to herself as the sled whooshed through the snow, the fur on her parka again almost covering her face protecting her skin from frostbite. *I wonder if my father had a dog team.* Goggles secured, she kept her eyes peeled in front of her watching for the plume of smoke Mitch described.

"There! There it is. The smoke," she yelled.

He patted her shoulder. "That's it all right," he yelled back.

"Mush, you huskies. Mush." Mitch stepped up the pace. He was eager to see his friend and patient again. The team responded making a controlled dash through the snow.

Drawing up to the cabin they saw Clarence shoot out the door sporting a graying beard and mustache. His salt and pepper hair was drawn into a braid falling to the middle of his back. He looked like a lumberjack with heavy boots, trousers that looked like they were heavily lined held up by suspenders over a red-plaid flannel shirt. A worn leather holster around his waist held a pistol.

"Whoa! Whoa!" The sled came to a halt. Mitch stepped on the brake, and rushed over to Clarence wrapping him in a bear hug.

"You're looking good, Clarence, you old goat. Wait til you see what I brought to you—a new friend."

"Yeah, well, looks to me like she needs help getting out of that harness you have her tied up in," Clarence said chuckling.

Mitch turned around and ran back to Melanie. "Sorry, let me help you."

"I thought I was okay then that strap got tangled," she said, reaching for Mitch's hand.

"There you go. Come on over and meet Clarence."

Mitch took hold of Melanie's gloved hand and they trudged back to the front door of the cabin where Clarence was standing. The sun was in Melanie's eyes, so she had to squint to see the bushman.

"Clarence, meet Melanie. She's been my traveling companion and lookout—first time on a dogsled and she spotted a moose."

"Hello, Clarence. Happy to meet you," Melanie said extending her hand. She was immediately enchanted by the bushman, his blue eyes twinkling back at her.

"Same here." Clarence grasped her glove with both of his hands. "Why don't you go on inside and get warm while I help Mitch here with the dogs. I'm sure they're hungry—he usually feeds them light when they're on the trail. Nothing worse than a team of sleepy dogs and I wouldn't want his *traveling companion* to freeze out here."

"Now Clarence, you fox. Yes, she's definitely more than a traveling companion," Mitch said beaming back at Melanie.

"I could tell. Mitch, I gathered some pine boughs for the team. Wasn't sure if you were bringing straw or not. Of course, if I'd known about your companion, I'd a known you wouldn't have room." Clarence chuckled as he and Mitch went to pound the pickets into the ground, lay the boughs, and then re-hitch the team to the pickets.

Melanie hesitated a minute, then decided to go inside and let the men have a chance to chat. The tiny cabin, built with logs, was very cozy. Three small windows were installed shoulder high. Pretty white-cotton fabric was tacked over the tops and held back with hooks, allowing the fabric to fall as a covering. A wooden platform, topped with a thin mattress served as a bed with room beneath for storage, and beams overhead for more storage or a place to dry firewood. A few miner's lanterns hung from the ceiling—one near the bed, another in the kitchen area, and one over a small pine table. A battery-powered radio and CD player sat on a small shelf next to the bed. She smiled, knowing that Mitch had purchased several cassettes as Christmas presents for his friend.

To the right of the front door was the kitchen space—a sink with cupboards on each side then a pine table. The wood stove provided a place to cook as well as extra heat. Several braided rugs cut the space into functional areas—kitchen, bedroom, and living room. There were no interior walls. The cabin consisted of one room. Melanie found it hard to imagine living in such a small space—no more than twenty feet by thirty, if that. On her way in she had seen tubs outside positioned to catch the rainwater off the roof. She surmised the water was gravity fed from the barrels into the cabin. In the winter, of course, the water froze so nothing came out of the faucet when she turned it.

Every section of wall served a purpose—shelving, hooks for Clarence's clothes, the bed, kitchen table shoved into a corner, and the stove. She wasn't sure where she and Mitch were going to sleep, but she thought maybe in sleeping bags in the middle of the floor—barely room for the two of them.

The team taken care of, Mitch and Clarence joined Melanie in the cabin.

"I've been looking for you, doc for the past day or so. But Christmas day. This is special."

The crackling fire inside the stove added to the cozy feeling between the friends.

"I like your cabin, Clarence," Melanie said standing by the stove warming her hands. "It sure gets cold here."

"Yeah—it got down to twenty below last night. Nice in the sun though—when she's up that is. Well you two make yourselves at home. I'll warm up some of my special moose stew I threw together in your honor—I thought for sure I'd see you yesterday, doc, but today the stew will be even better. Want some coffee or tea, Melanie. Pretty name, Melanie."

"I'm coffee'd out, but tea sounds wonderful."

Mitch pulled off his parka and sweater.

"We need to change, Melanie. I really worked up a sweat. How about you?"

"Yes, I checked my first layer while you guys were bedding down the dogs. It's definitely damp."

"Not much in the way of privacy in here," Clarence said chuckling. "A trapper and his wife came by—quite a spell ago—year or two maybe. Anyway, he fixed a curtain of sorts with a tarp back in the corner by those bookcases. Hooks are still there in the beams I believe. He laced the grommets with a rope over the hooks."

Mitch ambled over to where Clarence had pointed. "Hooks are here. Do you still have the tarp?"

"Yup—should be on the top shelf to your right. The rope, too. Tarp's green."

In short order, Mitch had installed a shower like space.

"Melanie, I'll go get the top bag, the one with the extra set of clothes in case we had to change on the trail. We can get into the dry stuff, have tea and then unload the sled."

"Want some help?" Melanie and Clarence asked in unison.

"What a couple of do-gooders," Mitch said. "I can handle it, thank you. You just get that tea going, Clarence."

Mitch returned, ushering in a blast of cold air. He dropped the bag in the middle of the floor and Melanie fished out a turtleneck T-shirt, fresh socks, and a pair of flannel trousers. Hustling into her little dressing room, she quickly changed into the dry clothes, putting her heavy sweater back over the top while Mitch changed standing next to the stove.

"Bring your wet clothes out here," he called to Melanie. "Clarence has a regular, top-of-the-line clothes drier set up."

"Will do."

Melanie joined the men and smiled. The collapsible, wooden contraption was just like the one her Aunt Helen hauled out for their wet towels when they returned home from the beach.

"Tea's ready. No cream but plenty of sugar. Mitch, did you bring me some powdered milk?" Clarence asked pouring the tea steeped nice and strong from a metal container of tea leaves dropped inside the pot.

"Yup. It's out in the sled."

"Did you build this cabin yourself?" Melanie asked taking a sip of the dark, steamy liquid.

"Me and some friends. When I retired I knew just where I wanted to live. Some of my buddies weren't so sure, but they came and stayed with me for a couple of summers before the big 'R' day. Slick as a whistle it was ready when I was."

"Was there a Mrs. Bettencourt in—"

Melanie was interrupted by the sudden barking of the dogs.

"What's that all about?" Mitch strode to the front door with Clarence on his heels. Melanie grabbed her parka and stepped out the door with them, closing the door behind her.

Chapter 44

THE DOGS were yelping. Barking. Jumping in the air. The roar of an approaching machine louder and louder. Mitch, Clarence, and Melanie stood just outside the front door, shielding their eyes from the brilliant sun bouncing off the white snow crystals.

"Looks like you're going to have some more company, Clarence. That's a snowmobile. Remember this morning, Melanie, I thought I saw something."

"Yes, but I didn't see anything."

Bursting from the line of pine trees, the man steering the noise maker slowly came into view.

"What the heck. That's Franklin Barrington," Mitch said.

"Who did you say," Clarence called out in alarm. "Franklin Barrington?"

"Believe it is, Clarence." Mitch took a few steps toward the approaching machine.

Clarence ran back into the cabin and emerged with a rifle, stuffing bullets into the chamber as he strode to Mitch's side. He raised his weapon and pointed it at the man climbing off the snowmobile.

"Clarence, for God's sake put that thing down. Franklin, are you following us?"

"Yeah. Tell your friend there to put his rifle down." Franklin began to walk toward the group. Thinking better of it, he stopped in his tracks. "What did you say your name is?" he asked.

Clarence backed away a few steps but kept pointing his gun at Franklin's chest.

"I didn't say. Now you get back on that contraption and go back where you came from. This here is my home. Do you hear me? My home!" he snapped. He took a step toward Franklin, moving the barrel of his rifle forward a few times indicating that Franklin should back up and leave.

Melanie's heart pounded. Words caught in her throat, as she backed away from the confrontation toward the cabin. What was going on. This nice old man had suddenly turned on Franklin. His anger filled with the fire of hate. Clarence meant business. His eyes narrowed to slits. His body coiled. His gun pointing directly at Franklin with his finger poised to pull back the trigger.

But Barrington stood his ground. He took a step closer to Clarence, peering into his face. His brow furrowed. His head bent slightly to his right as if to get a better look at the man pointing a gun at his heart.

In a whisper, so soft that Melanie wasn't sure she heard him right, Barrington uttered, "Artie?"

"You're mistaken. My name is Clarence. Now do as I say," Clarence yelled, punctuating his order by shooting in the air to the right of Franklin's ear just missing his shoulder.

Franklin didn't budge. He stood frozen. Melanie's breathing quickened. Did she just hear Franklin say Artie? She turned and looked at the man holding the rifle.

"Now look you two—stop this," Mitch said as he pulled his revolver from its holster pointing it to the ground. "Clarence, put that gun down. I don't know what's gotten into you two, but I'm not going to let either one of you do something you'll regret. Do you hear me, Clarence? Put the rifle down to your side."

Clarence didn't move. Squinting, he could see Mitch out of the corner of his eyes, but he didn't move his head. His rifle remained trained on Franklin.

Melanie tore her eyes from Clarence back to Franklin, his eyes puddling with tears.

Melanie suddenly broke away from the group, running through the snow to where Mitch had parked the sled for the night. Slipping on an icy patch, she fell to her knees. Righting herself she stumbled again, falling across the sled, throwing their bags, piece by piece, onto the snow. Uncovering her tote, she turned back to the men, her eyes seeing them very clearly for the first time. She ran slipping and sliding up to Clarence and fell on her knees in front of him as she tried to loosen the

Velcro strapping on her tote. The three men stood mesmerized by the antics of this seemingly crazed woman.

Melanie pulled out the contents throwing them on the snow. A sweater. A pair of heavy socks. A quilt!

Struggling to her feet, she carefully reached over and took the rifle from Clarence's grip and laid the quilt over his arm, looking into his eyes, questioning, tears now streaming down her face ... she knew the answer. This man was her father!

Chapter 45

ARTHUR BECKETT, his legs giving way, slumped to the snow staring down at the little quilt. He raised it to his chest, his eyes closed, then clutching the fabric to his face, hiding the anguish and pain he had endured every day since his precious Lorna Mae had been struck by a car, killing her … knowing there was no way he could take care of his baby … disappearing for the second time in his life rather than putting the baby in danger.

The danger! He jerked his head up and stared at the man he had run away from so many years ago. But this man standing before him had tears in his eyes. Arthur looked away from Franklin and back to the woman who called herself Melanie.

"What's your last name, my dear?" He knew the answer, for he was looking into the large blue eyes of her mother, Lorna Mae.

"Beckett," Melanie whispered as she knelt down beside him sobbing. He pulled her into his arms, the little quilt held between them … wrapping her as before, his baby daughter.

Mitch helped father and daughter to their feet and slowly guided the pair into the cabin. "Clarence, is it okay with you if Franklin comes in? Seems you too have something to settle. I won't leave you alone with him until you say so."

Clarence looked up sharply, through his tear-stained eyes. "Okay, but watch out. He's no good. He's evil. Don't trust him for a second. You hear me?"

"I hear you." Mitch turned Melanie to him, hugging her, rocking back and forth. He whispered in her ear, "You okay, sweetheart."

She nodded yes, unable to stop the tears from flowing onto his sweater.

~ ~ ~

MITCH LEFT them in the cabin stepping back outside. It was dusk, the temperature dropping. Franklin was sitting on his snowmobile, head down in his hands. Mitch trudged over to him and leaned against the handlebar. Neither man spoke. Franklin raised his head and looked up at the snow-covered peaks etched in gold from the sun now below the horizon. Mitch followed his gaze at the majestic yet treacherous mountain range.

"Doc, I was young and so foolish when Artie, Tommy, and I found the vein of gold that day. It wasn't until I was a much older man that I began to see things differently. I saw how wrong my father was. Wrong in the brutal way he treated people. I came to realize that the heavy burden I carried would never ease until I found Artie. I knew he was afraid of me, but the man he was afraid of no longer existed. To be honest with you, I thought Artie was dead. It wasn't until Melanie came looking for him, searching, believing in her heart she was going to find him alive that I began to believe ... believe there was a chance that, if I kept close tabs on her, I might find him, too."

Franklin slid off the seat then leaned back next to Mitch. He moved the toe of his boot back and forth on the snow, then looked up at the sky. Mitch, following Franklin's gaze saw an eagle soaring overhead unencumbered with its past as the humans beneath him wrestled with the results of their former actions.

"Do you think there's a chance that Artie, or Clarence or whatever he's calling himself, will listen to me?" Franklin looked at Mitch with pain-filled eyes.

"I don't know, Franklin. It's a heck of a situation. Doesn't seem the years have dimmed his feelings toward you any. I never saw such a mixture of fear and hate in a man as I did when he realized who you were. However, there is one thing I know for sure, and that is we should go inside before we freeze to death. Unless you want to leave now."

"Can't. I've come this far. I've more to tell him."

~ ~ ~

THE TWO MEN tramped through the snow to the front door. Mitch stepped into the cabin along with a puff of snow followed by Franklin who closed the door behind him. Arthur had lit the kerosene lanterns casting shadows in the corners of the small space. The fire in the stove hissed and crackled warming the air. Outside the wind picked up occasionally sending a spray of ice crystals against the window pane.

Melanie and Arthur were sitting at the table, hands held in a tight grip. Their conversation stopped when Franklin stood inside the door removing his gloves. Arthur coughed. Coughed again harder … and again … and again. A sudden spasm ripped through him. Unable to catch his breath the coughing strangled his windpipe.

Mitch ran outside calling to Franklin to come help him unload the sled. Hustling as fast as the snow and icy wind allowed, the two men finally had all the bags in the cabin dumping them in the center of the floor. Pawing through the heap, Mitch found the one he was looking for which held the medication he brought to Arthur as well as a new inhaler.

Arthur was now coughing up a black inky substance. Melanie darted to the sink picking up a cloth, dipping it into the remains of her teacup, and gently wiped his lips of the goo as Arthur, clinging to the edge of the table, tried to regain his breath. Mitch held the inhaler to his mouth and gently rubbed his back, coaxing the man to relax.

Arthur's body slowly responded and he leaned back in the chair. "Too much excitement, I guess," he said, still trying to fill his lungs with slow, rhythmic breaths.

Melanie patted his arm. He placed his leathery hand over hers, and, looking at her face, he traced her cheek with his fingers. "My baby girl."

Franklin picked up the chair by the bed and placed it next to Arthur's. Arthur shoved his chair back a foot, his right hand snapping to the gun in its holster. He didn't draw the pistol, simply stared at Franklin, a stare warning him not to push the fact he was in the cabin.

"Artie, there's no way I can change what happened after we found that gold. I—"

"You shoved Tommy. You killed him. I saw you and I was next. You wanted that gold so you'd be a big shot in your father's eyes. Another evil man." Arthur's words were filled with venom, but he didn't move from his chair, his hand remaining on the butt of his gun.

Franklin looked down at his hands, rubbing his fingers together, then up into Arthur's eyes. "I can't say I tried to reach out to save Tommy. My foot loosened the rocks. I just backed away. Tommy moved and the rocks gave way from the cliff. They gained momentum as more and more rocks cascaded—"

Franklin stopped, unable to talk. He sat staring at Arthur. Regaining his composure, he continued. "I looked up and you were gone. You were right to run. I panicked when I saw Tommy's twisted body far far down the mountain."

No one spoke. Only the crackle of the fire and the howling wind filled the silence in the little cabin. Melanie stepped to the stove, refilled the tea infuser with fresh leaves from the canister on the counter. She looked at the faucet—no running water. Holding the kettle up, she looked at Mitch, her brows raised.

Mitch took the kettle outside along with a large pot. He returned with both containers now filled with snow and placed them on the stove. Lifting her chin, he softly kissed her lips and then returned to sitting on the bed, watching the two men.

Franklin, leaning forward, both elbows on the table, looked again at Arthur. "I can't ever make it right between us, but I have to at least try," he said speaking softly. "I've drawn up a new will. One third of my estate goes to my son, Derek. One third goes to Melanie and one third goes to you, Arthur. In the event we didn't find you alive, your share would have gone to Melanie."

"I don't want your money—blood money. Do you hear me? I don't want your money. You think you're going to buy me off? You worried I'm going to sue you for what you've done? Nothing will change what happened—not your money, not your feeling sorry for—" Arthur pulled his gun out of the holster. "I should shoot you right now. Revenge for Tommy's death. But I'm not like you, Franklin."

Melanie looked at Mitch in alarm. He motioned for her to come to him. Taking her hand they went to the back of the cabin while the two men exchanged words—Franklin pleading for understanding and Arthur having none of it.

Mitch pulled out his cell phone and punched a code. "Dick, Dick, can you hear me? ...you're breaking up ...I need you to fly as soon as you can to the Bettencourt cabin ...yes, the one on the Susitna River ... where we went fishing last summer. I'm afraid someone is going to get shot. ...shot. Damn. The call dropped." Mitch pulled Melanie to him and whispered in her ear. "We have to try to talk some sense into them. They're both armed and there's no way Clarence ... I don't know what to call him ... is going to give up his gun."

"I know. You try to talk to them and I'll get that stew going. Maybe a little dinner will help. Mitch—"

"Yeah?"

"Call him Arthur. And—"

"And—" Mitch looked at her smiling face.

"I love you."

~ ~ ~

OUTSIDE THE howling wind covered the roar of an approaching snowmobile. The driver stopped on a ledge overlooking the river and a cabin below. He grinned, seeing the light shine from the cabin's window through his black ski mask.

Chapter 46

PERCHED ON THE LEDGE, Derek strained to get a better view of the little cabin below. A sudden blast of icy wind caught the snow in the trees over Derek's head coating his goggles and sending a chill through his body.

He turned off the engine of the snowmobile and doused the headlight. Cleaning off his goggles, he continued to look at the cabin, scanning the landscape surrounding it. He saw the sled, but not the dogs.

"Cussed animals are going to raise a racket when they catch wind of me," he muttered. "I'm going to have to take care of business fast. Like an ambush. Yeah, an ambush. Door's not likely to be locked, that's for sure. They won't be expecting a visitor."

Derek pulled out his flask of brandy and took a big gulp. The liquor warmed him when he swallowed, flowing through his system. He took another drink. "I don't have to kill the doc, or the bushman—just wound them so they can't chase after me. But Melanie … Melanie's a different story. No way can she survive. Have to make sure of that."

Derek squinted. Cleaned his goggles. Squinted again.

"I was right. There's a snowmobile beside the sled," Derek mumbled. He chuckled again at the thought of Melanie being dragged into the mountains if she'd tried to drive a team of wild huskies. He drained the brandy and threw the empty flask into the woods.

He adjusted his ski mask, wiped his goggles one more time, and checked that his revolver was correctly positioned in his pocket. He was glad he upgraded to a gun with six rounds. The gun was loaded and a second revolver was in his other pocket should he need it.

Satisfied he was ready, he gave the machine a blast of gas and began the descent to his quarry.

Chapter 47

TIGER WAS FIRST to hear the machine roaring through the trees. He rose to his feet out of the snow cocoon that covered him. He began to howl, nose in the air. In short order the rest of the team rose out of the snow shaking the flakes from their fur, each joining Tiger in sounding the alarm—yelping, barking, howling. The snowmobile slid to a stop in front of the cabin. The driver turned off the engine, charged the front door, and slammed it back against the wall.

Mitch, hearing the dogs, was on his feet and almost to the door. Melanie stood at the stove scooping the moose stew into the first bowl. Arthur sat at the table and Franklin sprang up to his feet. The masked man shot out the lantern over the bed then turned to the two men at the table.

"Dad? What are you doing here?" Derek hissed.

"I might say the same for you, Derek."

Mitch and Melanie turned back to the masked man.

"Derek?" Melanie said

"Put the gun away, Derek," Mitch ordered.

"You're on a fool's errand, Derek," Franklin said. "Do as doc says. Put the gun away."

"Ah, so you're all working together," Derek said waving his gun from one to the other. "Conspiring against me. Looks like I came just in the nick of time or Melanie would have stolen it all. Too bad Sid missed you in Florida, missy. Your demise at the hand of a hit-and-run driver would have saved me a lot of sleepless nights."

"You're too late, son. My will was changed last week and I signed it yesterday. Melanie and her father will each inherit a third of my estate. You'll get the other third."

"Gee, thanks, Dad. That's real gracious of you. But she hasn't found her father, or did you forget she's still searching? And there's the corporation. It's mine. All mine. Now why don't you go outside like a good boy. Get on that snowmobile and go home. We'll pretend this unpleasantness between us never happened."

"I think not, Derek," Franklin said. "I'm not going anywhere unless you come with me now.

Arthur stood up, and glared at the masked man. "Why don't you take off that silly mask and act like a man," he said.

"And just who are you to tell me to act like a man you sniveling little—"

"The name is Beckett! Arthur Beckett!"

"Well, well. Now that's real handy. I can eliminate the two of you at the same time."

Mitch inched towards Melanie. Another few feet and he would be off to the side but a little behind Derek.

"I wouldn't do that, if I were you, Derek," Franklin said standing in back of Arthur, but a step to the side facing his son. "If you persist in this little charade, there is one more piece of information you should know. Not only did I change my will, but the ownership of the company. In the event of my untimely death, the whole corporation goes to Arthur Beckett. And if anything happens to Arthur, it goes to his daughter, Melanie. You get nothing. Do you hear me? Nothing!"

"Oh, and why is that, Daddy dearest?" Derek said pointing the gun at Arthur. "You forget that I am the cosigner of all your bank accounts, your stock accounts, those silly CD's you insist on rolling over. By the time anyone finds your bodies I will be long gone."

Derek raised his gun.

"Nooo—" Melanie raced to her father knocking him to the floor as Derek pulled the trigger barely missing her as she went down. The bullet meant for Arthur hit Franklin in the chest. At the same time Mitch shot Derek in the shoulder. Screaming in pain Derek dropped his gun and immediately dropped to the floor to retrieve it.

Melanie, on top of her father, scrambled over the floorboards, reached for Derek's gun grasping it from his fingers just as Mitch stomped on his hand causing Derek to continue screaming out in pain.

Arthur unclipped his suspenders and with Melanie's help wrapped them around Derek's kicking feet.

Mitch ran to Franklin lying on the floor in a pool of blood.

"Doc. Doc, listen to me," Franklin whispered, his breathing labored. "Get Artie. Get Artie. I have to tell him. I have to tell him."

"Arthur, get over here quick. Franklin's calling for you," Mitch said, trying to stem the bleeding from his chest.

Both Arthur and Melanie crawled to Franklin's head. His eyes fluttered.

"Artie, can you hear me?"

"Yeah, I hear you, Frankie."

"Artie, forgive me. You have to forgive me."

"You're talking to the wrong man, Frankie. It's Tommy you want to forgive you."

"No. No. Artie, as God is my witness, it was an accident."

"What was an accident?" Arthur said.

"Your wife … the car … I killed your wife."

Franklin gasped. Clutched his chest, as his last breath left his body. He had said what he came to say. He was finally free and ready to meet his Maker.

Melanie and Arthur looked at each other, mouths hanging open in disbelief.

Mitch, tired of hearing Derek holler, tended to his shoulder wound. The bullet had pierced his shoulder and was bleeding badly. After applying a tourniquet around his upper arm, he searched in his medical bag and found a drug he could administer as a sedative knocking Derek out.

Mitch slumped to the floor alongside of Arthur, Arthur's arms holding Melanie. They sat surveying the unexpected turn of events, trying to process everything that Franklin had said during the course of the evening. Melanie, kissing her father's cheek, was the first to rise. She walked around the bodies of father and son to the stove, closing the front door as she passed. She took note that the dogs had stopped barking, and then did the only thing she could think of—started brewing a strong kettle of tea.

Mitch fished in his pocket for his cell, and punched the last number he had called.

"Hey, Dick. Can you hear me? … a better connection? Good. About tomorrow. Bring a body bag … yeah, that's what I said … and a stretcher for another man … and put out an arrest warrant for Sydney Jackman in Anchorage. What for? … Attempted murder of Miss Melanie Beckett, Daytona Beach, Florida. And, Dick, get to this cabin soon as you can. What's the weather report? … Clearing? … Bright and sunny! Thanks."

Epilogue

Wasilla, Alaska – Three Years Later

You are Invited to the
Grand Opening of the
Beckett, Baker and O'Reilly
Respiratory & Rehabilitation Center

July 7, 2:30 PM

THE LOBBY of the new respiratory and rehab facility was teaming with state officials, friends, community well-wishers, miners, and the press. The nutrition staff outdid themselves providing fresh bite-size crudités along with crackers topped with various versions of moose, caribou, and salmon. Roses, predominately in pinks, white and yellow adorned the serving tables. Coffee, tea, and a fountain of lemonade were available to quench the crowd's thirst as they waited for the press conference to begin.

"Melanie, do you think I should change my tie? Maybe this blue one would be better and it matches your dress ... and your eyes," Mitch said. A smile crossed his face as he kissed his wife.

"Darling, it wouldn't matter if your tie was adorned with jumping salmon, everyone is waiting to hear you speak and to shake your hand. I still can't believe you talked Aunt Helen into flying up with Cindy. And, yes, I think I do like the blue one better."

"Did you hear her last night at dinner," Mitch said. "That was brilliant of you by the way to seat her next to Arthur. Anyway, I almost fell off my chair when she told him it was nice to see him again, but she still wasn't totally ready to forgive him for leaving you. I think her words were, 'let bygones be bygones,' or something like that."

With a soft rap on the open door, Aunt Helen, dressed in a dark blue suit, entered Mitch's office. "Hey, you two, it's time to go downstairs."

"Thanks, Helen, we'll be right down. Where's Arthur?" Mitch asked.

"That man's impossible," she said with a smile. "He and that Gus person are in the nutrition center counseling some of your new patients on how they're going to eat from now on. Not how they should eat, mind you, but, how they're going to eat. He did say he'd give them a pass on the Brussels sprouts. See you downstairs."

"Tell the two of them I want them at the press conference now. They can finish their counseling later," Mitch called out to her as she left. He changed his tie and took one last look in the mirror and then turned to the woman standing beside him.

"Melanie, when we were married you insisted on a plain band made from the gold your father had panned when he was a young man. "Today is the official beginning of the rehab center which you have worked so hard to make a reality." Mitch reached into his light-gray suit pocket, fingering the object he had put there waiting for this moment. Withdrawing his hand, he took hold of her left hand and slipped on a three-carat solitaire diamond set on a gold band, fashioned from the same gold as her wedding ring. "Thank you, my sweetheart, for bringing to life your husband's dream. I love you with all my heart."

"Oh, Mitch, it's beautiful." Beaming, Melanie looked into her husband's brown eyes, his reddish hair with a few strands of gray, and thought he was the most handsome man in the world. "I love you too, my darling."

Clearing his throat, Mitch said, "I think we'd better go to that press conference, Mrs. O'Reilly."

Hand in hand they walked down a winding staircase to the lobby, and into a small auditorium, shaking hands as they made their way to the staging area and up to the podium.

"Welcome, everyone. Arthur, will you come up here with us, please."

Arthur, sitting in the first row next to Helen, Gus, and Cindy, turned red.

"Come on, Arthur," Helen said. "You're a member of that family. Now get going."

Arthur did as he was told, and stepped up on the platform next to Melanie. She took his hand and gave it a quick squeeze along with a peck on his cheek.

"Now, sugar, enough of that," he whispered beaming.

"Thank you everyone for coming," Mitch said. "Members of our staff are here to take you on a tour of this new facility and to explain why the three main areas are so important to the future health and well-being of our mining community, but also to those suffering from respiratory ailments throughout the lower forty-eight. Nutrition, exercise, and learning how to fight respiratory disease—be it from inhaling coal dust or cigarette smoke as two examples—are vital to improving and maintaining the patient's quality of life. So, please, take the tour to better understand what the Beckett, Baker, and O'Reilly Respiratory Rehabilitation Center is all about. Are there any questions?"

"Dr. O'Reilly, who is Baker?"

Mitch reached for Melanie's hand and held it tight. "Scott Baker was a miner. He was a patient of mine and became a dear friend. We hunted and fished together, but more importantly we talked for hours about black lung disease and how the miners, who fell victim to it, could help themselves. He died three years ago at the age of sixty-nine. He died of black lung. He left everything he had saved from his years down in the mine, $48,000, to me as seed money to build our dream—this center."

"Mr. Beckett, I understand Franklin Barrington left his considerable fortune to you and your daughter. Would you tell us how that came about?"

"Frankie and I worked as young lads in most of the coal mines around this area—Houston, Palmer, Sutton, Healy ... well, I worked at Healy. Frankie ultimately went to work for his father. When he met his untimely death ... I'm sure you've all been reading about his son Derek's trial, let's just say it was his way to ask forgiveness from all of us, not just Melanie, Mitch, and I, but you out there as well, for some of the, well the bad deeds the Barrington's perpetrated on us over the years. It's quite fitting don't you think that it is their money, added to Baker's seed money, that built this center."

"Thanks, Arthur. I think that about sums it up," Mitch said, shaking his father-in-law's hand.

The crowd stood applauding then began exiting the auditorium. Reporters gathered in front of the stage asking more questions, microphones in hand. A photographer from the Anchorage Daily News muscled his way to the front.

"Dr. O'Reilly. Dr. O'Reilly, can you and Mrs. O'Reilly and Mr. Beckett step away from the lectern so I can get a picture for the front page of the newspaper?"

"Sure. Melanie, Arthur." Mitch moved to the side of the stage.

"Wait a minute," Melanie said, as she scampered off the stage to where Cindy was sitting holding a baby in a little quilt. Melanie picked up the two-month-old baby, and carefully walked back up onto the stage to Mitch and her father. She placed the baby, her blue eyes open wide and wrapped in the quilt from the wooden box Melanie found, into Arthur's arms. The baby waved her hand out of quilt fingering the gold locket hanging on a chain around her mother's neck. Melanie kissed the baby's fingers and then turned to the reporter. "Please meet the newest member of our family, our baby girl, Lorna Mae."

The End

REVIEW REQUEST

Please consider leaving an honest review. Reader reviews are the lifeblood of any author's career. For a long-ago typewriter-jockey like myself, getting a review (especially on Amazon) means a lot.

It's easy. Log into Amazon, search for the book. **TAP** Customer Reviews at the top of the page. **Click**: Write a Customer Review.

Thank you!

ADD ME TO YOUR MAILING LIST

Please shoot me an email to be added to the list for future book launches:

MaryJane@MaryJaneForbes.com

Website www.MaryJaneForbes.com

Acknowledgments

Thanks to Zoya DeNure and John Schandelmeier for their tips. Their business, Crazy Dog Kennels, provides everything to do with sled dogs: winter tours, boarding, dog sales, Alaskan Store, and the Iditarod. Visit their website (the pictures alone are worth a look):

http://www.dogsleddenali.com/AlaskanAdventures.htm

Roger and Pat Grady continue to dive into the first drafts of my manuscripts mining the pages for grammatical errors and inconsistencies in the plot. Once again, their efforts made for a much cleaner book and story.

As ever, thanks to Vera Kuzmyak, Lorna Mae Prusak, and Adele Fatigate for their initial feedback and catching pesky errors.

Thanks to my daughter, Molly, who somehow squeezes a review of my manuscripts into her very busy life.

Cover design: by Angie: pro_ebookcovers

~ ~ ~

Dear reader, as you settle back in your comfortable chair, I hope you'll enjoy meeting new friends and how their lives are impacted by the situations with which they are confronted. Alaska is an amazing state.

Author Notes

MARY JANE FORBES: The Baby Quilt is a work written with love. Her father worked in the Alaskan mines as a young man. Her research followed his footsteps by car, plane, and dogsled.

THE BABY QUILT was Mary Jane's seventh novel. Her passion for writing grows as her readers urge her to give them more stories. Retired, she has the freedom to pursue her fifth career, a writer.

Stay tuned at:

www.**MaryJaneForbes.com**

The Baby Quilt

Copyright © 2011 by Mary Jane Forbes

ISBN: 978-0-9827488-8-6 (sc)
Printed in the United States of America
Todd Book Publications: 3/2011
Port Orange, Florida

Made in the USA
Lexington, KY
10 July 2019